D1326906

WITH AND WITHOUT BUTTONS

Also by Mary Butts from Carcanet
The Crystal Cabinet: my childhood at Salterns

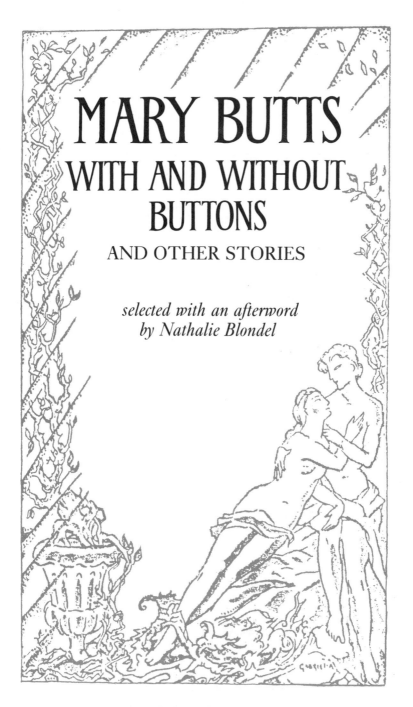

MARY BUTTS
WITH AND WITHOUT BUTTONS
AND OTHER STORIES

AND OTHER STORIES

*selected with an afterword
by Nathalie Blondel*

CARCANET

First published in Great Britain in 1991 by
Carcanet Press Limited
208-212 Corn Exchange Buildings
Manchester
M4 3BQ

British Library Cataloguing in Publication Data
Butts, Mary *1890-1937*
    With and without buttons and other stories.
    I. Title   II. Blondel, Nathalie
    823.914 [F]

    ISBN 0 85635 944 0

The publisher acknowledges financial assistance from
the Arts Council of Great Britain

Set in 10½pt Ehrhardt by Bryan Williamson, Darwen, Lancs
Printed and bound in England by SRP Ltd, Exeter

The editor dedicates this selection to
Paul Evans
in memory of his sense of humour
and zest for life.

Contents

Speed the Plough

He lay in bed, lax and staring, and obscure images rose and hung before him, dissolved, reshaped. His great illness passed from him. It left him too faint for any sequence of thought. He lay still, without memory, without hope. Such concrete impressions as came to him were sensuous and centred round the women of the hospital. They distressed him. They were not like the Kirchner girls in the worn *Sketch* he fingered all day. La Coquetterie d'une Ange. One need not know French to understand Coquetterie, and Ange was an easy guess. He stared at the neat counterpane. A tall freckled girl with draggled red hair banged down a cup of cocoa and strode away.

Coquetterie, mannequin, lingerie, and all one could say in English was underwear. He flicked over the pages of the battered *Sketch*, and then looked at the little nurse touching her lips with carmine.

'Georgette,' he murmured sleepily, 'crêpe georgette.'

He would always be lame. For years his nerves would rise and quiver and knot themselves, and project loathsome images. But he had a fine body, and his soldiering had set his shoulders and hardened his hands and arms.

'Get him back on to the land,' the doctors said.

The smells in the ward began to assail him, interlacing spirals of odour, subtle but distinct. Disinfectant and distemper, the homely smell of blankets, the faint tang of blood, and then a sour draught from the third bed where a man had been sick.

He crept down under the clothes. Their associations rather than their textures were abhorrent to him, they reminded him of evil noises...the crackle of starched aprons, clashing plates,

9

unmodulated sounds. Georgette would never wear harsh things like that. She would wear...beautiful things with names... velours and organdie, and that faint windy stuff aerophane.

He drowsed back to France, and saw in the sky great aeroplanes dipping and swerving, or holding on their line of steady flight like a travelling eye of God. The wisps of cloud that trailed a moment behind them were not more delicate than her dress....

'What he wants, doctor, to my mind, is rousing. There he lies all day in a dream. He must have been a strong man once. No, we don't know what he was. Something out of doors I should think. He lies there with that precious Kirchner album, never a word to say.'

The doctor nodded.

He lay very still. The presence of the matron made him writhe like the remembered scream of metal upon metal. Her large hands concealed bones that would snap. He lay like a rabbit in its form, and fright showed his dull gums between his drawn-back lips.

Weeks passed. Then one day he got up and saw himself in a glass. He was not surprised. It was all as he had known it must be. He could not go back to the old life. It seemed to him that he would soil its loveliness. Its exotics would shrivel and tarnish as he limped by. 'Light things, and winged, and holy' they fluttered past him, crêpe velours, crêpe de Chine, organdie, aerophane, georgette....He had dropped his stick...there was no one to wash his dirty hands.... The red-haired nurse found him crying, and took him back to bed.

For two months longer he laboured under their kindness and wasted under their placidity. He brooded, realizing with pitiful want of clarity that there were unstable delicate things by which he might be cured. He found a ritual and a litany. Dressed in vertical black, he bore on his outstretched arms, huge bales of wound stuffs. With a turn of the wrist he would unwrap them, and they would fall from him rayed like some terrestrial star. The Kirchner album supplied the rest. He named the girls, Suzanne and Verveine, Ambre and Desti, and ranged them about him. Then he would undress them, and dress them again in immaculate fabrics. While he did that he could not speak to them because his mouth would be barred with pins.

The doctors found him weaker.

Several of the nurses were pretty. That was not what he wanted. Their fresh skins irritated him. Somewhere there must still be women whose skins were lustrous with powder, and whose eyes were shadowed with violet from an ivory box. The brisk provincial women passed through his ward visiting from bed to bed. In their homely clothes there was an echo of the lovely fashions of *mondaines*, buttons on a skirt where a slit should have been, a shirt cut to the collar bone whose opening should have sprung from the hollow between the breasts.

Months passed. The fabric of his dream hardened into a shell for his spirit. He remained passive under the hospital care.

They sent him down to a farm on a brilliant March day.

His starved nerves devoured the air and sunlight. If the winds parched, they braced him, and when the snow fell it buried his memories clean. Because she had worn a real musquash coat, and carried a brocade satchel he had half-believed the expensive woman who had sat by his bed, and talked about the worth and the beauty of a life at the plough's tail. Of course he might not be able to plough because of his poor leg...but there was always the milking...or pigs...or he might thatch....

Unfamiliarity gave his world a certain interest. He fluttered the farmer's wife. Nothing came to trouble the continuity of his dream. The sheen on the new grass, the expanse of sky, now heavy as marble, now luminous; the embroidery that a bare tree makes against the sky, the iridescent scum on a village pond, these were his remembrancers, the assurance of his realities. Beside them a cow was an obscene vision of the night.

Too lame to plough or to go far afield, it seemed as though his fate must overtake him among the horned beasts. So far he had ignored them. At the afternoon milking he had been an onlooker, then a tentative operator. Unfortunately the farmer recognized a born milkman. At five o'clock next morning they would go out together to the byres.

At dawn the air was like a sheet of glass; behind it one great star glittered. Dimmed by a transparent shutter, the hard new light poured into the world. A stillness so keen that it seemed the crystallization of speed hung over the farm. From the kitchen chimney rose a feather of smoke, vertical, delicate, light as a plume on Gaby's head. As he stamped out into the yard in his gaiters and corduroys he thought of the similitude and his mouth twisted.

In the yard the straw rose in yellow bales out of the brown dung pools. Each straw was brocaded with frost, and the thin ice crackled under his boots. 'Diamanté,' he said at last, 'that's it.'

On a high shoulder of down above the house, a flock of sheep were gathered like a puffy mat of irregular design. The continual bleating, the tang of the iron bell, gave coherence to the tranquillity of that Artemisian dawn. A hound let loose from the manor by some early groom passed menacing over the soundless grass. A cock upon the pigsty wall tore the air with his screams. He stopped outside the byre now moaning with restless life. The cock brought memories. 'Chanticleer, they called him, like that play once...'

He remembered how he had once stood outside the window of a famous shop and thrilled at a placard.... 'In twenty-four hours M. Lewis arrives from Paris with the Chanticleer toque.' It had been a stage hit, of course, one hadn't done business with it, but O God! the London women whose wide skirts rose with the wind till they bore them down the street like ships. He remembered a phrase he had heard once, a 'scented gale'. They were like that. The open door of the cow-shed steamed with the rankness that had driven out from life.... Inside were twenty female animals waiting to be milked.

He went in to the warm reeking dark.

He squatted on the greasy milking stool, spoke softly to his beast, and tugged away. The hot milk spurted out into the pail, an amazing substance, pure, and thick with bubbles. Its contact with caked hides and steaming straw sickened him. The gentle beast rubbed her head against her back and stared. He left the stall and her warm breath. The light was gaining. He could see rows of huge buttocks shifting uneasily. From two places he heard the milk squirting in the pails. He turned to it again, and milked one beast and another, stripping each clean.

The warm milk whose beauty had pleased began to nauseate him. There was a difference in nature between that winking, pearling flow and the pale decency of a Lyons' tea jug. So this was where it all started. Dimly he realized that this was where most of life started, indifferent of any later phase. 'Little bits of fluff,' Rosalba and all the Kirchner tribe…was Polaire only a cow…or Delysia?… The light had now the full measure of day. A wind that tasted delicately of shingle and the turf flew to meet him. The mat on the down shoulder was now a dissolving view of ambulating mushrooms.

'Yes, my son,' the farmer was saying, 'you just stay here where you're well off, and go on milking for me. I know a born milkman when I see one, and I don't mind telling you you're it. I believe you could milk a bull if you were so inclined….'

He sat silent, overwhelmed by the disarming kindness.

'See how the beasts take to you,' the voice went on. 'That old cow she's a terror, and I heard you soothing her down till she was pleasant as yon cat. It's dairy work you were cut out for…. There's a bull coming round this forenoon…pedigree…cost me a bit. You come along.'

As yet they did not work him very hard, he would have time to think. He dodged his obligations towards the bull, and walked over to an upland field. He swept away the snow from under a thorn bush, folded his coat beneath him, and lit a cigarette.

'And I stopped, and I looked, and I listened.' Yes, that was it, and about time too. For a while he whistled slowly Robey's masterpiece.

He had to settle with his sense of decency. It was all very well. These things might have to happen. The prospect of a milkless, meatless London impressed him as inconvenient. Still most of that stuff came from abroad, by sea. That was what the blockade was for. 'I've got to get away from this. I never thought of this before, and I don't like it. I've been jockeyed into it somehow, and I don't like it. It's dirty, yes dirty, like a man being sick. In London we're civilized….'

A gull floated in from the sea, and up the valley where the horses steamed at the spring ploughing.

'A bit of it may be all right, it's getting near that does one in. There aren't any women here. They're animals. Even those girls they call the squire's daughters. I never saw such boots…. They'd say that things were for use, and in London they're for show…. Give me the good old show….' He stopped to dream. He was in a vast circular gallery so precipitous that standing one felt impelled to reel over and sprawl down into the stalls half a mile below. Some comedian had left the stage. Two gold-laced men were changing the numbers on either side. The orchestra played again, something that had no common tune. Then there swung on to the stage a woman plumed and violent, wrapped in leopard skin and cloth-of-gold. Sometimes she stepped like a young horse, sometimes she moved with the easy trailing of a snake. She did nothing that was not trivial, yet she invested every moment with a significance whose memory was rapture.

Quintessence was the word he wanted. He said…'There's a lot of use in shows.'

Then he got up stiffly, and walked down the steep track to the farm, still whistling.

When the work was over he went out again. Before the pub, at the door marked 'hotel', a car was standing, a green car with glossy panels and a monogram, cushioned inside with grey and starred with silver. A chauffeur, symphonic also in green and bright buttons, was cranking her up. Perched upon the radiator was a naked silver girl. A woman came out of the inn. She wore white furs swathed over deep blue. Her feet flashed in their glossy boots. She wore a god in green jade and rose. Her gloves were rich and thick, like moulded ivory.

'Joy riding,' said a shepherd, and trudged on, but he stood ravished. It was not all dead then, the fine delicate life that had been the substance of his dream. Rare it might be, and decried, but it endured. The car's low humming died away, phantom-like he saw it in the darkling lane, a shell enclosing a pearl, the quintessence of cities, the perfection of the world.

He had heard her voice. 'I think we'll be getting back now.' She was going back to London. He went into the bar and asked the landlady who she was.

'Sort of actress,' the landlord said. And then, 'the war ought to have stopped that sort of thing.'

'Why, what's the harm?'

'Spending the money that ought to go to beating those bloody Germans.'

'All the same her sort brings custom,' the wife had said.

He drank his beer and went out into the pure cold evening. It was six o'clock by the old time, and the radiance was unnatural.

He walked down the damp lane, pale between the hedgerows.

It widened and skirted a pond covered with vivid slime.

'And that was all they had to say about her....'

He hated them. A cart came storming up the hill, a compelling noise, grinding wheels and creaking shafts and jingling harness; hard breathing, and the rough voice of the carter to his beast.

At the pond the horse pulled up to breathe, his coat steamed, the carter leaned on the shaft.

'Some pull that.'

'Aye, so it be.' He noticed for the first time the essential difference in their speech.

Carter and horse went up the hill. He lit another cigarette.

Something had happened to him, resolving his mind of all doubts. He saw the tail lights of a car drawing through the vast outskirts of a city. An infinite fine line went out from it and drew him also. That tail lamp was his star. Within the car a girl lay rapt, insolent, a cigarette at her lips.

He dreamed. Dark gathered. Then he noticed that something luminous was coming towards him. Down the hollow lane white patches were moving, irregular, but in sequence, patches that seemed to his dulled ears to move silently, and to eyes trained to traffic extraordinarily slow. The sun had passed. The shadow of the hill overhung the valley. The pale light above intensified its menace. The straggling patches, like the cups of snow the downs still held in every hollow, made down the lane to the pond's edge. It was very cold. From there no lighted windows showed. Only the tip of his cigarette was crimson as in Piccadilly.

With the sound of a charging beast, a song burst from him, as, soundless, each snowy patch slid from the land on to the mirrored back of the pond. He began to shout out loud.

'Some lame, some tame, some game for anything, some like a stand-up fight,
Some stay abed in the morning, and some stay out all night.
Have you seen the ducks go by, go a-rolling home?
Feeling very glad and spry, have you seen them roam?
There's mamma duck, papa duck, the grand old drake,
Leading away, what a noise they make.
Have you heard them quack, have you heard them quack, have you seen those ducks go by?
Have you seen the ducks go by, go a-rolling home?...'

The way back to the farm his voice answered Lee White's, and the Vaudeville chorus sustained them. At the farm door they forsook him. He had to be coherent to the farmer. He sought inspiration. It came. He played with the latch, and then walked into the kitchen, lyrical....

'And I stopped, and I looked, and I left.'

A month later found him on his knees, vertical in black cloth, and grey trousers, and exquisite bow tie. A roll of Lyons brocade, silver, and peach, was pliant between his fingers as the teats of a cow. Inside it a girl stood frowning down upon him.

Despair was on her face, and on the faces of the attendant women.

'But if you can't get me the lace to go with it, what am I to wear?'

'I am sorry, madame.... Indeed we have done all that is possible. It seems that it is not to be had. I can assure mdame that we have done our best.' He rose and appealed to the women. His conviction touched them all.

'Madame, anything that we can do...'

The lovely girl frowned on them, and kicked at her half-pinned draperies.

'When the war starts interfering with my clothes,' she said, 'the war goes under....'

His eyes kindled.

Friendship's Garland

There are days when the worst happens so completely that the whole consciousness is dyed to the particular colour of the abomination, when escape is impossible, and one plays rabbit to the world's weasel with just a little bravado, no courage, and no sense of style.

We were caught that day in Zoe's bedroom full of flowers, arranging our hair. We had forgotten that we were the hunted and innocent. They had been after us for a long time. We knew that they were after us; but we were younger, quicker, and more impudent; only too young. We could not believe that, in the end, they would not come and eat out of our hand. Perhaps they will, but only by exhaustion, not by persuasion, and that will not be good enough.

Among other things, they wanted to take away our lovers, not because they wanted them themselves, but because they could not love themselves, and naturally disliked it that we could; and there was money in it, and fear of us. At least, we liked to think there was fear. But chiefly it was virtuosity in the creation of pain, and that we did not understand. 'What do they do it for?' said Zoe. 'Never mind. I know they've got their knife into us. The great thing to do is to keep them in a good temper, and never trust them at all.' You see, we could not get rid of them; they had seen to that.

Then we began to laugh, and make little traps to annoy the blind animals who were following us. Keen noses and no eyes. Intelligences without imagination. Zoe arranged a little bribe of flowers. I could see them smell it – and soon it would be out on the dustbin. They were not people who burn their dead flowers.

17

'It will look pretty and civil. It will keep them quiet a little,' she said; 'but they don't know how strong I am when I mean to get my own way.'

Indeed, I hoped they would find her strong. She was a better fighter than I, but she could not make herself invisible. That is my long suit.

In Zoe's room we could see trees waving over a wall. The summer wind was moving them, and below us there would be tea, and great, silent cars moving so pleasantly in the street. The white staircase of the house was like the easy stairs you fall down in dreams.

The telephone rang by Zoe's bed. I heard a man's voice speaking from any distance, from no distance, from a place outside the world. He spoke a great deal. I heard Zoe say: 'Yes, Carlo, of course we'll come,' but his voice went on, and I was reading a book when she said to me:

'They want us to meet them, and I said we would. Who says we're afraid?'

'Where?' said I.

'At the Craven. Where Carlo can pretend that he's a man of the world.' That made us laugh. We ran about Zoe's room, taking alternate turns at the mirror, and calling 'Carlo' and 'Craven' to one another till the door opened and his sister ran in. We could not think how she had got there. It was like an annunciation or a burglary. I felt she would be followed by the servants she had run past. She wanted to do her hair and show us her hat. It was a tight, evil hat of scarlet leather. I re-set my sombrero, and Zoe hung a little veil across her eyes and took her downstairs, and we got into the car. Carlo was repeating, 'The Craven. We'd better go to the Craven. I've got some news for you, Zoe.' I lay back and watched the streets slip past.

We stood about the steps while Carlo fidgeted with the car and tried to make the commissionaire recognize him. He tipped him a wink, he was haughty, he confided in him, he gave him half a crown. He was attended to with the others, but still Carlo hung on, and would not be done with it. His sister was impatient: 'Oh, Carlo,' she said, 'let's go in and leave him to it.' Willing enough we were to leave him to it, and wasted no embarrassment on her.

Through the noise and the iron streets, even through the racing wind the sun poured, roaring its heat through the wind at the huge buildings and the crowd. Those are the hours when the city pays for being a city, and is delivered over to the wind and the sun and their jackal the dust. All the earth pays, but principally the city. On the other hand, inside the Craven there is no nature at all. These things are not natural, marble like cheese, red velvet, and plaster gilt.

We sat down. Carlo was a long time seeing about his car, and when he came he was petulant because we had not waited for him, and had ordered tea. Only for a moment. He never thought of anything for more than a moment. He was quite safe to forget. Only he always remembered again, and a little differently, so that he could always escape on a misunderstanding, and pick up the line again and again and again. He bounded across to us, and flung himself into a cane chair, petulant, pretty, and artful, and his sister deprecated him while they were both hunting. I knew. It was Zoe they were after today, and they had not expected to find me at her house. I could lean back and watch and eat éclairs. They were too sweet, and I got sticky. Then I could smoke in the rich, stale quiet whose murmur was like the tuning-up of birds that never would begin to sing.

Zoe wore a pearl, hung from a piece of jade, on a chain spaced with small pearls. Cosmo had given it to her. Carlo saw it: 'I say, Zoe, d'you know you're wearing Celia's pearl?' Celia had been Cosmo's first wife, and we had hoped she was now reincarnating as something reasonably intelligent and plain.

Zoe answered in her small, distinct voice:

'Yes, his father brought it back when they looted the Summer Palace.'

The brother glanced at the sister, who looked as though she could eat it, and Carlo said: 'I only mean – you don't mind my saying this, Zoe? – that I don't think Cosmo thinks it's worth much. I was going through some papers from him the other day, and he hasn't insured it. Of course, it suits you.' His sister laughed, and lifted it off Zoe's breast with her pink paws whose dimples felt like rubber. She said:

'I expect he's left it to his daughter. Anyhow, I'm afraid she'll think it ought to be hers. I don't envy you, Zoe, once you're married, with that young lady.'

'She shall have it as soon as she's old enough to wear it,' said Zoe.

'You are quite right. But you know in seven years – she'll be eighteen then – will you want to give it to her? We always mean to behave well. But jewels are jewels, and flappers are flappers. It becomes you perfectly.'

Zoe lifted her small, apricot-brown head. 'In seven years we shall be so rich that I shall have all the jewels I want.'

I sorted this. First of all, the thing wasn't real, and later there was going to be a row about an artificial gem. Of course those two, I added to comfort myself, hadn't the wit to choose or the money to buy an ornament like that. It had been left to Cosmo's daughter, who was preparing – who was being prepared – to hate Zoe, who was to be her stepmother. Wasn't it real? It looked real. I wanted to lick the pearl to try it – I did not like to do it then and there.

Carlo's sister said: 'I don't know if you've thought of it yet, my dear, but I should send that child off to school. A good convent would be about the best. If you keep her there most of the year, she won't see so much of the Travers. She spends all her time with them now, and they don't like you –'

I protested – 'Oh, not convents. They save you the trouble of teaching it manners, and that's all.'

'Manners maketh man,' said Carlo, who had not been to Winchester. I looked away spitefully, and saw his sister register both slips.

'What did Mrs Travers say about me?' said Zoe steadily.

'You know what she is,' Carlo hurried up, all anxious friendliness. (His attack was to dance up and down and give tongue, while his sister hunted soundless, ready to spring.) 'They want to keep Cosmo for themselves. They make a lot of money out of him. Travers thinks his wife had an affair with him once. Anyhow, you know how people are jealous. She's awfully attractive, Zoe, and she'd like to do you in.'

In the mirror in her bag Zoe looked at her face, brown, painted, celestial, a mask to set dark crystal eyes and hyacinth-curled hair.

'Yes,' she said stubbornly, 'but what did she say?'

A remark like that is pure science, the investigation of a fact. I was pleased.

Carlo answered: 'Only that Cosmo's a bit older than you.'

'Oh, be quiet, Carlo,' said his sister; 'it's not as serious as that. At any rate you can be sure of one thing, the Travers would sooner die than fall out with Cosmo. It would lose them half their business. People in their position can't afford to say what they think. That's a very effective check.'

And admiration and honour and affection? One has heard of these as reasons. Only today we have to find out what is the reality for which these words are the correspondents. It was tolerable when we used to say the words and go ahead on the emotion they evoked, but now one has not the courage to say them any more.

'Come off it, Carlo,' said I; 'you're inventing the whole thing.' If Cosmo quarrelled with them, would Carlo get the business? To be put away for future observation.

His sister said: 'Don't you think that the test of success is to be in a position not to know people? After all, like all the arts, the art of life ought to consist in a series of eliminations – the Farrells, for instance. I am always telling Carlo not to know the Farrells. People like that do one harm. You never know what harm people will do.' Carlo fidgeted.

'I tell you I've dropped them.' And then – 'Don't you see, Zoe, that one has to be careful? The world's a rum place, and people do such impossible things.'

Zoe, who should certainly have learned something about science, said: 'Which of my friends do you mean, Carlo?'

'Who d'you want to be rid of now?' said I.

Carlo tapped my knee. 'You know, Cesca, some of our set are impossible. Dennis, for instance, and his brother. It does one no good to be seen with them. They are *mal vus*, you know.'

'One can't afford it,' said his sister. 'Things get about, you know.'

'What things?' said Zoe.

'It is very difficult. Of course that is not their real name. My cousins are furious about it. It is not quite right to trade upon other people's position.'

Dear me, those boys were my cousins too. They'd always been called that. Acquitted, after a gasp – the dears! 'Really,' I said, but still feeling shame, and too proud to defend them. They were my dear friends, but I suspected them of needing defence. And did not know how to defend them. Then I remembered that Carlo and his sister hardly knew them at all.

'Cosmo adores them,' said Zoe, 'and helping Cosmo is my job.'

'You'll have your work cut out,' cried Carlo, pulling one of her curls with his rapid familiarity. 'And talking of Dennis, Cesca, guess who I saw him with last night?'

'My husband, I suppose,' I said.

'That's it. They were at the Pomme d'Or, and I can tell you they were getting on with the brandy. Pippa was with them.' Carlo's sister laughed.

'Young wives like us have to put up with that, I suppose.'

And why shouldn't they go to the Pomme d'Or and stand each other drinks? I saw my life through a dingy glass. These people had made me ashamed and afraid. They were also my kin. I must lose them and could not. The effect of shame and fear was to rearrange every physical object that I could see. The Craven turned into a temple built of cane and plaster, oily marble and velvet, and I observed the cult there. To be rich – to be *rangé* – to be cute; to cut your friends – to suffer for nothing – to be a cad. Carlo and his sister suffer. They were priests there, and I hoped a sacrifice.

All the same, I was afraid of their temple. Zoe was chattering about where she and Cosmo would live when they were married.

'There's a lovely house in Lower Seymour Street – we could just afford it. It has such a room to dance in. Anyhow, I'm to have it.'

Carlo shouted: 'I advise Cosmo not to touch it! Doesn't he know that Van Buren has bought all the houses along there to pull them down in two years? That's why they're going cheap.'

'Don't bring down the walls,' said his sister with her good humour.

But I became suddenly afraid of a pillar with a gilt mask on it that might be coming at us, while Zoe and I were being fattened on éclairs and listening to this and burning our mouths out with cigarettes.

Zoe rubbed out the stump of hers and refused another. So did I, thinking I must find a gesture of my own. Well, I was out of gestures. I wanted to hide. I wondered what religion would do for Carlo and his sister. Then I reflected on what it had done, and saw religion like an anæmic girl, like Peace in a foreign post-War cartoon, not attempting to keep this cretinous juggernaut on a lead. I thought of the Polis, which appeared clean but feeble. I wanted a sanctity to turn on like a tap. I felt myself growing old, my face greasy and stretching under its make-up. Then we left.

Outside, the wind knocked us about. It blew me into a Tube, and up north on the back of a shrieking noise. At the end of the Tube the trees were rocking in a wind that wrapped itself round me and flung me down a steep road.

'So that is what happened down there,' I said, 'and I am running home to hide.' That is life. That is the world. The wind is doing its best for me. Home is good enough, but a little austere, because one is always at work there.

I noticed that it was evening. Then I heard the old trees. I crossed the wide road and saw it was empty, and came alongside the house, and went into its dull, dark porch and let myself in.

In an instant I knew the house was empty. 'They' were all out. 'They' never troubled me, but they had gone away. I went into my room and saw the trees. The afternoon had gone over its crest, and was falling downhill into evening. In my room the walls were white, and went up to the ceiling like a pure sky. I saw my own things, coloured wood and polished wood, a Persian duck painted gold and scarlet, a green quicksilver ball.

I saw my face in a mirror, grown old. I had not chosen that. I stripped my face of its make-up, and combed my hair into a straight short piece. The wind marched in from the balcony, and dying in the room, it died outside, until there was no sound but that of the oldest of the trees turning. Then it was renewed. Not a cat came in. I lay on a bright shawl and listened to the tunes of the house. Every room had a tune we had taught them, and under our tunes was their tune, which I had sometimes heard, but could not learn; though I think I moved to it when I did not think at all. I did not think of us, nor of the mummy upstairs, nor of the wireless set or the flute, nor that in the room next mine lived the most beautiful child in the world, nor of the seven glass balls for the seven planets that hung in the room downstairs. Or of the cat that threaded the rooms, or the green bath-salt in a jar upstairs.

I listened a long time to a song like the noise made by the

footfall of cats, and when I came out of listening to it, I saw the room take fire. Point and point and point that could reflect took light. The low sun covered my face with fire. Outside the leaves were fiery green tongues. The white walls soaked it in and waved it back, so that, when there were not steady points, there were cloths of fire. It was cool. I pulled a fur over me. The fire took the colour of each object, and presently they began to move, and I swung with them. Out we sailed, and I knew that I was conscious of the movement of the earth through space.

I got up and crossed the room and went out on to the balcony that ran round the wall of the house, above the garden where the dandelions were in seed and in flower. There came a roar of wind that flattened me against the walls, and I knew the house was a ship plunging through the sea. The trees were racing us, and a small moon beat up against us up the sky.

When I came back, and looked in the glass again, my face was half old, like a child's recovering from a sickness. I lay down again, and turned on the light beside my bed, and read a book about the Greek Polis which now sounded like a fine folk-tale.

But almost at once I went to sleep. When I woke, the wind had gone again. It was night. Houses at the end of two gardens were pure gold inside. I saw them through black leaves. My light was out. But the great tree had come in and stood on the threshold of my balcony. It did not menace me. It was absolutely silent. But it said: 'I guard your door. This place is tabu. Keep tabu.' When I saw the branches pass in and point at me, I did reverence to the tree and its precinct; and when I could have knelt on the floor in awe of the tree's sanctity, I saw that it was also myself; and when I got up and looked into the glass again, I looked like a child that has been dipped in dew.

The House-Party
To Jean Cocteau

H e wanted to go and stay with them, in the sea-washed, fly-blown, scorched hotel along the coast, whose walls were washed primrose above the blue lapping water, where one mounted to bed by a plaster stair outside above the shifting sea, under the stars shaken out in handfuls.

There might be peace there. Under Vincent's wing a man could stand up a bit. Vincent was English, tender, serious, older than he. Vincent wanted him to come. Was no doubt cajoling, hypnotizing away certain objections. Objections that were always made about him, especially by his own countrymen, the Americans who made a cult of Europe, a cult and a career, not quite perfect in their transplanting, and conscious of it. As he was conscious of the virgin energy and high intelligence which made them a reproach to him. Also, that in certain directions, his adventures outnumbered theirs as the stars the dim electric-light bulbs of the hotel. No they would not want him, and Vincent, poor fish, would sweat blood to fix it so as not to annoy them. And at the same time risk his old friendships on his behalf. A fool, but a sort of a glorious one. Glorious fools pay. Meanwhile he would go – and not be a nuisance to Vincent. Take a back seat all right. Give Vincent what he had to give. An audience, someone to *play* with. Worship carefully disguised. If Vincent bored him.... An essential meanness in the boy reminded him how he could take it out of Vincent, Vincent who was standing by him; not out of Vincent's friends. A cracked little specimen of a gigolo, after a year in prison for something he had not done, his comfort was to be revenged on the good. Vincent would pay.

Great André also was staying there; the silver hill, the lance-point of the boy's world. Vincent would present him. He would have something to worship as well as Vincent. Make Vincent jealous? No, no, no. Perhaps he'd find out how to behave as they behaved. No, no, no. God help him, he'd play no joy-boy tricks.

He had met Vincent at the Casino of the great town, and had heard about the fun they were having, the harmonious, mischievous house-party ten miles along the coast.

'International relations going strong. I'm still on speaking terms with Dudley and Stretton, Winkelman and Marjorie, Edouard and Clarice; with America, Mittel-Europa, England, and France. And since André came I've never had such a time or known such a chap. Like lightning and Mozart.'

Not a word about the social lift André's presence implied. Only response to his longing to be there, and a little diffidence.

'Dudley and Stretton are difficult, Paul. Tastes very definite and standards unaccountably high. It works out that they don't like anyone who isn't in the arts, or pickled in New York, or else extremely important socially –'

Paul said: 'I'm a pickled New Englander. That's to say that I'm of much better family. But you can tell them I won't interfere. They won't even see me except across a room at meals. I suppose they can stand that. If I come, it's to see you – I know what's due to people who have been kind to me.'

Vincent smiled. 'I see a good deal of André. I expect you'll meet him too. I'll take you a room for tomorrow, and when the high cultural atmosphere of Dudley and Stretton gets a bit too much we'll amuse each other –'

Paul saw him leave the Casino and shoot across the bright gardens to find his car – a young man whose large bones the flesh covered delicately, who, even indoors, set the air stirring. Not noisy at all, but easy, as if his life was nourished by a fountain, whose very deep waters rose and sunned and spread themselves evenly, and mounting kept everything they touched astir. Paul, shooting craps at a bar, remembered a sentence Vincent had quoted, 'The generosity of strength', supposed Vincent had it, and his heart felt the little nick of pain which was his form of worship; he knew that he did not mind saying, even to Vincent's face, that Vincent was his superior.

A moment later he began to reflect on his simplicity. These

scrupulous Englishmen were easy to make. Because of their innocence, because of the insolence implied in 'the generosity of
strength'. He counted the knuckles of his small, rosy, gold-wired
hands, tried the pointed nails, jerked up the arm to feel the bicep,
who had once been an athlete, looked in the mirror at his pretty
clothes and handsome childish head, spoke to the barman in
faultless French. To reassure himself. It was all he had to take
over there to people disorderly with treasure of mind and spirit.
Of bodies also, but he knew how to exploit his –

Vincent, rushing his car along the hill coastline, was saying
that the ill-used brat should have his treat.

He had acquired Paul in a moment of occupation with human
wrongs. The boy had been handed over to him by another man
as a hopeless case. It had seemed to him that Paul's life of dissipation, malice, and despair, occasionally touched by a kind of
nipped sweetness which flowered only into unwilling loyalty, was
one form of a universal condition, a rot nibbling at a generation.
This gave him the power to illustrate the particular by the general,
translate the boy into boys, and take valuable notes. His feebleness
lay in an observation he had shirked: that all Paul's qualities, his
vices, his sincerity, his aspirations, and his affection had been
steeped, as though his body in filth, in some essence of the sordid
which made him repellent. Apart from the blindness of generosity,
a connoisseur in bad smells might have accepted the handsome
lad, courteous when he liked, ravenously grateful for scraps, and
rather chic.

Vincent looked out to sea, over jade dancing, called it a drawing-room ocean after the Atlantic, and kicked himself mildly for
ingratitude. If only Paul could be dipped in it and brought out
clean. He knew that what he needed was purification, from what
corruption he did not quite understand. He concentrated too
closely on the horror spot of the story. The boy's imprisonment
for folly; his desertion by his friend. The savage sentence; the
appalling illness that had released him; the details of his third
degree. Little Paul naked and terrified, and beaten up. Questioned to insanity; flung for weeks into a filthy cell; chained to a
black murderer running with sores. He had infinite pleasure when
Paul responded, told him how peace of heart and self-respect
ran in like small tides 'into the mess it has made of me. Don't

suppose that when I'm with a person like yourself, it doesn't do good to my character –'

Vincent knew that behind the small admission there was a continent of waste land and reserve. Also that it was sincere. Paul brought him presents, a cigarette holder in almost good bad taste; a popular fiction that had impressed him; once, God knew how acquired, a lapis snuff-bottle stoppered with coral, the most gentlemanly chinoiserie, full of oily, permanent eastern scent. Paul loved to give, loved himself for giving. Vincent was touched. He enjoyed presents too. They played with them together. Vincent was persuaded that Paul did him good, not by exercising him in charity, but by taking him out of his group intensities. Paul had lively adventures, good because they were ordinary debaucheries. Yet in each there was something distasteful, as though the prison and the hospital had left a taint and a sepsis. The sea racing below on Vincent's right was the sign of purification. For purification was necessary. A saturation – in what? Vincent did not exactly know. He only knew an essence that washed his spirit daily as the sea his body, the wine in his throat, music in his ears. What was it? He resisted the easy race temptation to call it by old names, religion, God's grace, because they had once been counters for it, possibly were so still. But observing great André with his crowd of lads, who came for an hour, for a day, flashing in and out of the Frenchman's darkened room, a word had crystallized out for such activities. *Kourotrophos*, a bringer-up of boys. Not much more than one himself, Vincent brooded its meaning, half-ashamed of its emotional charge, the humility and elation it brought him. If he could not show Paul the Good, he would bring him samples, rub his nose in them if necessary, pitch him, kick him into it, scrub him. Hold him up a glass to see his restored cleanliness. For the spiritual-sensual reward: to hear Paul say that it was good, clean and on his knees. And see the little thing run off translated, his small gifts liberated, reasonably at peace.

Beside the classic sea, the classic title took form: Kourotrophos. He saw Cheiron, Pallas. In the same land, built of gold and violet rock, barren, but *'a good nurse for boys'*, André; the dead Scots officer who had licked him into shape. He meant to try a practice hand on Paul; for someone in the future, the friend of friends, who at the start would need that. Paul was just a try-out, with a dash of affection in his sentiment towards him, and a slight kick.

Vincent was an English type, mutely convinced that he was there for a purpose, accepting the discipline of the virtues as preparation for an unknown. A particularly unknown unknown at this time, with religion and love and pride of land and race off the map, and the unconscious the cheerless substitute. Meanwhile he had to be observant, study the iron puritanism in which Paul had been raised. Was that the soil which had grown his corruption? He decided finally that it had only set the stubborn will that resisted catharsis. They had read together the story of the Butcher of Hanover, and he had noticed that the horrible fairy-tale had struck Paul with terror. Also that it had excited him. Which suggested a Hoffman in Paul? Really, really. But Vincent had spent an hour or so of his imaginative life in the old quarter of Hanover, in and out the over-hung, cobbled passages and crazed buildings, greased and glazed with old blood; still alive, this time with painted, emotional boys, followers of men's oldest profession. Current hysteria, gossip, intrigue, on a medieval stage. Mystery of stairs that lead nowhere and doors that do not shut, and round the corner to Augustus' Live Wire Bar.

Throw fire, crystal, salt between little Paul and that place, where Vincent could have strolled and picked up wisdom; where the absence implied the presence of his lord. He left his car at the hill garage and ran down the terrace stairs of the small town, past gay, plaster houses roofed with round tiles, along slots of cooled, highly seasoned air; a ribbon of liquid sky on top; and at the end of each stair a patch of still water, divided by masts, the basin of the little, prehistoric port, till he reached the hotel on the quay. He had Dudley and Stretton to appease, where, from his point of view, appeasement should not have been necessary; and it is hard to entreat those we love. He could foresee the iron stare at Paul's name, the lip-twitch of contempt, and, incidentally, the glance of apprehension.

He ran up the white, sea-cracked stair and knocked at André's door. In bed, God bless him, in a room where the sea-light sifted through wooden slats; the red silk of his pyjama coat falling back up dark ivory arms. Ready for any emergency. Ready always to talk. As by magic, he spoke immediately of Dudley and Stretton. 'Any news from the Upper House, *mon cher?*'

'I've news for them,' said Vincent. 'Listen, André, I've a *déclassé* little friend –'

'You always have – so have I. Well?'

'– I put it to you, André, the boy ought to come. You'd think that, after his past, his countrymen would be hunting him round with bouquets –' He tried to find the French for scapegoat.

'*Bouc émissaire*,' said André. 'I don't suppose they chose a valuable beast.'

Then it was like a ride on a wave, repose on the sea's back, when the Frenchman said: 'I will arrange it – he has a right to stay where he pleases – Dudley and Stretton can't have everything their own way. Leave it to me.'

They embraced, and Vincent felt as if the sea had lifted him gently on to a firm beach.

In another room of the hotel Dudley and Stretton's sails emptied a moment and they flapped in a pocket of the rising gale they were running before to well-earned fame. Vincent had said 'check' when he had gone straight to André to sponsor this deplorable specimen of their native land. In their sun-steeped rooms, filled with objects of comfort, utility, and impeccable taste, they yielded to distress. Dudley picked at the typewriter, Stretton sat on the edge of the bed. The sea danced at them. They were saying that no European ever could or ever would understand the way rumour reached New York, and booked its passage by return of liner under new and horrible disguises. That people would talk; that people might say they were friends with the boy if they were seen in the same place. It was all very well for André, a prince of the arts, and for Vincent with his shameless English indifference to public opinion; they had extra cats to whip. Stretton was tall, fragile, ageless, beautiful. Dudley was handsome, quick, serviceable. The pair two formidable hunters, out for the lion's share. In the civilization of Europe, kind, ruthless, observant pioneers. Neither aware of the power of their arms, the prestige of their fresh strength. Both aware that Vincent had put their queen in danger, intentionally or not.

Dudley clattered off a letter on the typewriter. Stretton put on a record. *'I ain't Nobody's Darling'* pointed the situation. He took it off and substituted Mozart. Perhaps not perfectly appreciated, the lovely air flowed out above 'the hard hearts of men'.

The day after, while André took a cat-nap after two hours' unbroken lunch conversation, Vincent hurried along the sea-bordered rock-path to the station. In the train Paul soiled his hands, clinging to the black-dusted rod in the corridor on his way. The train ran into a tunnel, into the mountain that rushed down to the edge of the dancing beach. In an instant he had passed out of flashing air into brownness, into hell's neck, after a paradise of blue stone-pines. The boy suffered in it, and from more than fear that its filth would soil his smartness. To his literal, primitive fancy it was like what hell would be, hell where he'd been before, hell where he belonged. Only this tunnel had an end, which ran full into a station, where Vincent was waiting for him beside more sea.

Together they left hell's mouth, Paul trotting a little behind Vincent's stride, and glad to run to earth in his sunny room and arrange his pretty properties. It occurred to Vincent, as he watched him displaying trifles, that there were people without house or land, with a dressing-case and a photograph frame for anchor. Paul said: 'I suppose you couldn't get me a window table downstairs? I can promise you not to look at Dudley and Stretton. Or rather I shall leave it to them. They can cut me or not as they please.'

'I've fixed that for tomorrow – André asked you to dine with us tonight.' He saw Paul start, harden, and then sitting on his bed drop backwards, his forearm over his eyes.

'What is it, lad?'

'I don't know; but you take me out of hell into heaven. It's all you. I know that. I'll kiss Dudley and Stretton if you like.'

Vincent jumped. That wouldn't do. Keep 'em apart. Quite simply, because he was ashamed of Paul. Also he remembered their iced politeness when they had seen him once before, the night he had taken Paul to one of their parties, when he had been at fault, and Paul had acted in character. 'Let them be,' he said; 'you can make friends with them later.'

'You mean,' said Paul, 'that I may be fit to know them later?'

'I mean that if you clean up and cheer up you can meet them later on your own ground.'

At dinner Paul sat by André, at the head of the table, opposite Vincent. Beside him an Englishwoman, neither ugly nor old, who had Dudley beside her; and by Vincent, Stretton; and by him a pretty, watchful French girl. The long table, with a Frenchman at the head of it, which was the hotel's show-piece and alarm. An annoyance and bewilderment for the old soldiers and older maids who filled the *salle à manger*, when the conversation rose above the clash of plates and the shifting of the sea.

J'ai du commerce sexuelle
Avec mon colonel
J'ai connu, charnellement, mon commandant –

seven gay voices sang when the courses were late. The English-woman was teasing André, who was whittling green olives into improprieties. As Paul passed a carafe he was nodded to by Stret-ton, and asked where he had been, as though his address had been a public lavatory, and he given a chance to conceal it. It was like being let out on parole. No, it was not parole, it was freedom. He told them all a story, suggested by André's anatomical recon-structions of the olives, and they were silent.

He felt walls closing on him again. Like the walls of his prison that his body had somehow got out of and left the rest behind. He was listening now to their talk. About the same thing as his story, but excused because the words were different, and mixed up with implications he didn't understand. That was cleverness: that was hypocrisy. They were like bright flies hatched out of dung, and he the beetle content to roll its ball. He thought about that until he caught André's voice again, half-way through a tirade on the theatre. He hadn't seen the play. Coolly Stretton asked for his opinion. Again, what he said was not *like* what they said. He flushed. André sheltered him. Stretton illustrated André's criticism with a New York production. He was analytic, weighty. By chance, wrong on detail. Paul corrected him eagerly. Silence. With a pinch of assurance gained, he invited André and Vincent to the café on the quay. André refused gently. Vincent carried him off.

The little town was built on terraces chipped out of the moun-tain flank, between two precipices, round whose base even the Mediterranean flung itself in spray. It was very still in the little port, white docks ran in sideways along stale emerald water, an utter security for little boats. The quay stones, salt-bleached and fretted smooth, where the cables rubbed, were laid with rust-coloured nets. Eternally torn, eternally repaired, untidy girls in black gowns, with black-brown necks and dusty, dark curls, mended them. But at this season, at night, the open bay looked as if it were divided by a wall, pierced with round holes, blazing with circular light, behind which could be heard voices and music; the space between the wall and the quay shot across by launches, turning and tearing, ripping the water's green back; and little ceremonies of recommitment to land or sea took place on the quay, as the commander of the battleship welcomed or was welcomed. And every room along the front or up the terraces roared with sailors, their pockets full of money; and the town girls out with them to supply the honey; and nine months later, after the christening of too many grey-eyed, flax-haired babies, the Curé would get out his annual sermon on the sin of fornication, until the next season brought more ships from newer and richer lands.

But from the day the ships arrived one could observe the girls' black overalls and dingy espadrilles shed, to be replaced by wall-paper cretonnes and shoes whose high heels turned over unaccustomed ankles; and shiny, pink wood-fibre stockings over olive legs. While the gramophones worked to death, and the tin pianos beat out jazz, and the cars of arriving and departing officers swept light paths on the bent road up the hill.

Much later the noise became more concentrated by the water's edge, more expressive of the emotions of drunk men struggling with a foreign tongue. Finally the ship police would load them into boats, groaning; the last cargo would shoot out, to be replaced at dawn by men with fresh leave and stragglers returning from the great town where Vincent had refound Paul. It had not occurred to him that it might be more than a spectacle for an American *deraciné* to see the men of his fleet out on a spree. Only he noticed a difference in the quality of their pleasure. He was at a play of which Paul had seen the rehearsals. Might at any moment run off behind the scenes. For Vincent the play was just sufficiently amusing; but Paul had imported something with him from the great town, where half the earth swarmed up and down an esplanade, where each vice had its location, and even the lamp-posts and bicycles were over-sexed. Sailors talked of the swell joints and the swell girls they had found there. Paul stood the drinks. He was sparkling with excitement. The sombre child, alternating at dinner between timidity and impertinence, changed into a sharp-eyed lad in the know.

For some days before, as well as for some nights, Vincent had observed a shadow about the quays. First because it had tried to sell him an obscene book, then because it tried to sell André an obscene book, then because it tried to sell everybody an obscene book. Then because it was obscene. Of no race or of any; grey, green, greasy, with a few horned teeth and black nails; its clothes a patchwork of hotel leavings, its speech a kind of American, pronounced with a lisp, the chi-chi of the East. Referred to as the Pimp. No name, no associates, it would appear and be gone. It knew a whore-house, a cinema. Lived by finding the people who wanted those places. Found them. Of no age. Probably an immortal. Vincent, composed of west wind and tree sap, the wine, beef, apples and classic literature of an English country house, was affected by him as by a bad smell. In the café he went over to speak to Stretton, escorting the little French girl. Danced with her once, introduced her to a sober, charming sailor, turned and saw Paul, leaning along the bar with the Pimp. Stretton must have seen him. Anyhow, he pulled the boy's shoulder round, surprised at the shock inside himself.

'What d'you mean – speaking to that filth here with us?'

Surprise from Paul might have cut his fury; defiance justified it – but the boy said: 'No, no. Please take me away. It was not my fault. He spoke to me. I'm afraid of him.'

The man glanced, cringing at them, and began to melt away, merging into the crowd at the door.

'Don't play into Stretton's hand then.' Thoroughly cross he replaced him at the table.

Timidly Paul looked up at him. 'I couldn't help it, Vincent. I saw him once or twice about before. I don't quite know what he is –' Then as 'All right. Tell me why you're afraid of him' framed in Vincent's throat, the child's notes went out of Paul's voice, and the self-conscious, self-righteous debauché spoke: 'Why should I mind what Stretton sees? If you're ashamed of me, you've only got to say so and I'll go –'

'Say go,' said a guardian angel tartly to Vincent. As generally happens, he told it to shut up. In fact, 'Shut up' was all he said aloud to Paul.

'Pan,' said Vincent, on a terrace on the top of the world, overlooking the sea in which some day Solomon is supposed to drown it, 'what's Pan to you?'

'I guess,' said Paul, 'he's my god.'

He seemed to want to hear something about him. Vincent sketched the varieties of his cult. He did not neglect him as a god of sex, but down the gulf below them a yacht race was standing in, on blue-roughened water, the true wine-dark, a handful of silver slips. And as he watched them, all that was natural in his training and imagination made him breathless with love. Inattentive and unprepared later to meet reserved sarcasm from Paul – 'That's all I know about Pan – what's your idea?'

Paul's answer was the smile of contemptuous pity a novice might get from a nasty old priest.

'I could show you a bit more about him if you came with me up the back streets at night.'

'Only drunks and drunks and more drunks. Like the Prince Regent's waistcoats.'

'There's more than that – you'd see how people get away with it – what can I do –' The dark blue stone eyes were shining again; his smile to himself, an acute sensuality outside the romantic attitude to sex. Vincent whisked the car back down the hair-pin bends and wished it would grow wings, fly away with Paul and punish him, and show him a life so different that back streets or high hills would be Tom Tiddler's ground to him. And it felt as though he had exchanged a cake of soap stuck with nails for a crystal ball when he joined André after dinner, alone.

Then Stretton came in. He said, 'Where's your interesting experiment, Paul Martyn?'

'Out somewhere, I suppose. I'm not his nurse.'

Then they listened to André, brought their lives to illustrate his. They loved him.

Dudley knocked. 'I've seen your Paul below. He asked me why I was ashamed to be an American. I didn't know that I was.'

Vincent did not understand their problem. The hag of unspecified bad conscience hobbled in. André was tactless.

'He will not make a scandal for us here, will he?'

'Of course not. And he asks rude questions out of defence. Let the boy enjoy himself his own way. What reason is there to turn him into a bad copy of us?'

'By all means,' said Stretton. 'A glimpse into the mentality of the Pimp at secondhand might be useful.'

Vincent felt an impulse to go down, fetch Paul, and beat him. Both ways Dudley and Stretton cramped his impulses. And for nothing would he miss an evening of André's magic mind.

Very much later he looked out his bedroom window, high up over the slip of cobbled square. Dancing was over and carouse and rows. On the other side of the hotel the sea lifted quietly up. Here and there a window of the old town showed a square, rose or orange. Somewhere a concertina gasped a dying breath. A line of plane trees rustled, and drew a delicate shadow on moon-whitened stones. Out of the house shadows an occasional cat slipped. He washed himself in the moon-quiet. Then saw that there were two people about, presently visible in the open square – Paul and the Pimp. At the foot of a stair they turned and mounted quietly together up the town. Vincent stayed still. So that was what Paul did when he went out to play. Follow him out and ask to be taken to see Pan? The shadows seemed to be coarsening and thickening. He remembered the smell of thyme – sweet, rank, classic grossness. He cleaned his teeth a long time. The stuff was called euthymol. A whiff of magic about; great indifference to Paul. He slept.

Paul woke late next morning, and with the nervous anxiety common to his race began to feel for symptoms of disease. Throat sore, mouth 'like the bottom of a parrot's cage', nerves no worse than usual, but outside scrutiny. Normal awakening under abnormal circumstances. He should have been rather pleased with himself, but part of his conscience was raw and in raving protest. He hadn't come to Vincent to behave like that. Hated Vincent for the stab of remorse which made it necessary to suppress tears. The spasm passed and he smacked his lips. Stretton wouldn't have dared go where he'd been, and Vincent wouldn't have cared. And André. He bet André knew more about it than he'd let on.

All the same, he hadn't meant to keep the rendezvous he had made with the Pimp at the bar before Vincent had turned him away. Why in hell had he? Why in hell shouldn't he?

He got up, groomed himself with concentrated attention, and went out. At the tip of the breakwater, under the pepper-box pharos, André and Stretton were sunning themselves. Paul had on the coat he had worn the night before. A pocket crackled. He pulled out a sheaf of dirty drawings and sat down to re-peruse them. The breeze blew one along. Stretton retrieved it, glanced at it, and rose politely to return it. Impudence seized Paul. He walked back with him and showed the whole lot to André then and there. André laughed; but both were embarrassed by Stretton. High intelligence and boundless information uncorrected by wide experience takes all comfort out of criticism. But because André laughed and chattered, Paul thought he had triumphed. Would not let his sexual curiosities drop. Again he bored them. André finally let him see it, and was told in French too rapid for Stretton that there was no need for him to play the prude. He lay sprawling by André, his tight, smart looks displayed beside the worn seraph, laid out, light as blown steel, among the stones. Blind with need for response he became reckless, using '*tu*' and calling the Frenchman by his first name. Knew himself further and further separated from him, until he yelped from his starved little heart:

'D'you know, André, you seem a hypocrite to me. When you were younger you raised enough hell. You're getting affected.'

André, infinitely wise and unwise, whose memories were of Paris, poetry, the adventure and passions of a unique personality, did not want to be reminded of his incomparable adolescence. How it could be visualized by this little animal. He raised himself on his elbows and began an apostrophe on aeroplanes, men, birds, bird-priestesses and the hawk of Horus. On wings. Stretton tossed back the thread as it wove over Paul's fair head laid comfortless on his small, clasped hands. He held hard to the belief that all they said was only his own life dressed up. It was because they weren't honest and had read things. Suddenly he got up and almost shrieked at André: 'If you'll excuse me, I'm going. I can't stand any more. *Ta voix m'agace.*' Stretton made a gesture. André carried on, his voice the minutest division of a tone higher.

He lunched with Vincent. It had been agreed that Vincent

should leave the long table, to which he had not been reinvited, and join him for one meal each day. His outburst at André, his failure with André, had let loose a storm of sensibility and a need to confess. Vincent was cold. Paul began to explain again how good Vincent was for his character. It was a dreary shock when the Englishman said: 'Then what were you doing out last night with the Pimp?'

He saw the boy retreat into himself, trapped. Then plaintively: 'I can't speak to you now, Vincent. Leave me alone, please.' He saw Vincent shrug his shoulders, unaware of the pity which could have won him forgiveness.

Vincent went to fetch André, Dudley, and Stretton for a run in the car. Found André on his bed talking, supported on his elbows, and morally by Stretton. After Paul's small, musical drawl, French tired his ears. He was oddly unstrung. Paul's presence, which could not separate him from André, divided him from Stretton. All three whom he loved, and differently.

Stretton said: 'Paul has told André that his voice gets on his nerves.'

The pit of Vincent's stomach made itself noticeable. 'What's it been about?' A few careful sentences, terrible in their scrupulous avoidance of condemnation, gave the meeting on the quay. Stretton holding his mirror up to nature. A superb mirror, reflector also for his petulant, stern beauty. He might as well have struck Vincent when he left the room to tell Dudley the car was ready. Vincent looked at André, to watch his mouth set in its divine smile. It did not. He turned over nervously.

'Vincent, let me speak frankly. Before your *protégé* came, and Dudley and Stretton were so perturbed, I had thought them unjust. I meant, in fact, to take the boy up. To give him the run of this room. See if one could help him. Teach them a lesson in kindness. I see now that it is impossible. To begin with, he is a bore. Bores are unhelpable. Then he is corrupt. Not on account of his life or his taste in art. And I rather liked him when he said that my voice got on his nerves. It gets on mine. I am speaking of the quality of qualities.'

Bitter-crystal waters of lucidity. Vincent nodded. 'But, André,' he said, 'I had him here on trial. I know now it is no good. I'll send him away.'

'Not at all on my account. It is you I am considering. You let your heart run away with you. The boy adores you, but some day he will play you a dirty trick. You don't know these little boys as I do. And you English play the *grands seigneurs* in a world that does not admit their existence. And –' (the clause was flashed in) 'I do not want any scandal here.'

Very well punished, Vincent said: 'All right, André, I'll clip his poor little claws. I shan't cut him myself because of what happened to him in prison when he was a child. I hold that because of that a lot should be forgiven him. We'll run up into the mountains. I'm going for the car.'

'Nasty pill,' said Vincent, stopping in the corridor to feel his wounds. So much for the Kourotrophos. He had risked André and Stretton on that piece of swank, and had been very properly put in his place. Was it for that he was nearly weeping? Not at all, he observed, sufficiently a pupil of the French mind; but because his little kouros could not be brought up. Would never *put off the old man like a garment.* The filth had gone too deep, he was dyed in it. Vincent knocked at Stretton's door.

'Coming?' There was discussion in the further room.

'Dudley wants to know if there will be room.'

'Yes, for the four of us.' Dudley appeared, perfect, neat, complete, hands in pockets, his look pitched straight at Vincent. He did not mean to come if Paul were asked. And he was perfectly right.

Worse luck. They were perfectly right.

'Only us four. Are you coming?'

'Yep.'

They dined on another terrace-rock, hung over space; a cloud hiding the gardens and vineyards of men. All that was visible was other stones, staring like animals at the shifting, glittering sea. They sat until the sun turned its dancing-floor into a lacquered parquet, a gold path for his dip into the ocean baths.

Vincent told them the memories of Atlantis, Hy-Brasil, the Apple-land. André told them about Basques. A Basque and what had happened to him swimming in the Basque country. A story which would have pleased Paul.

The boy spent an afternoon chewing the cud of stale excess. Inclined for company, he went down to the hotel front, on the quay; and there, as though newly risen from the dead, was the Pimp, pestering a tourist. And when he had pestered him, he made straight for Paul, sat down beside him, and carried on, as though it had never been interrupted, their conversation of the night before, held in a dim-lit maroon-hung brothel of the old town. There followed suggestions how they might be useful one to the other.

'You gotta pull on plentee smart guys. You bringa them to me.'

In bright gold daylight. The only creature who wanted to speak to him. Misery rose in Paul. The man became a spectre of his imprisonment: of all that cut him off from other men. He was a louse out of his filthy cell, who had crossed the water on his body: fattened on his secretions. The rich pleasure he had taken in the man became a fearful punishment to him, who believed in punishment: who had been punished. As he stared away from him, the green harbour water plaqued with gold, the old stones tufted with wild flowers, the fringed mountains against the low sun, all the shapely, brilliant beauties of Europe's cradle became alive with obscenity; neutral forms for the foul to make plastic. His very precious ring, the gold snake with the diamond sunk in its head, was a small fiend in command. A late fisherman landed a net of flapping, dying, sea-people; snatched a small squid from the salt-running pile and held it up. Once Vincent had caught one – Vincent so easy and happy out in boats – and had told him how they were motifs for decoration on Cretan jars. An awful people they must have been. Between the squid, the Pimp, and his little ring he was being damned alive. He could not tell him to go. He must go where he was bid, as before he had gone to prison. A Calvinist ancestor appeared.

'My great-great-grandson, it pleased the Lord to damn you before you entered your mother's womb. It is so, even though you should learn humility and bless Him for it.' The squid's arms writhed. The fisherman, young, gay, beautiful, held it up; flashed his white teeth at the small crowd round him, lowered his head and bit till the eight arms fell limp. Lifted his slimed face and laughed. Paul, now nearly mad, shrieked.

The Englishwoman walked along the quay, looking for friends. She saw Paul and smiled at him. He staggered up, agonizedly produced the pretty manners of his upbringing.

'Come and have a drink with me,' she said; 'are Vincent and
André back yet? You didn't go with them?' The Pimp faded.

'No,' he said; 'I'm afraid I've offended them.'

'English people ain't easy to offend. It's your American nerves.'
He looked to her also like a child. 'What have you been up to?'
she said.

'Vincent is angry because I spoke to that man. I didn't mean
to. I'd give anything to get away –'

'You've only to cut him and he'll run.'

'But you didn't know. I can't.' She saw that it was serious.

'Vincent told me something. If you want to live differently, you
have only to tell Vincent. He's patient –'

'God knows I am sorry, but what's the good?' All the same,
when he looked round, the harbour was again a place for ships.
'Thank you,' he said, 'most people are decent to me now. And
when they aren't, I dare say it's my fault.'

They dined together, waiting for Vincent. But by the time he
returned, Paul disintegrated again. The Englishwoman spoke to
Vincent: 'Go and look after that kid.' Vincent, only half-willing,
found him in his room; heard only a petulant, self-righteous
harangue on Vincent's misconceptions about him – which he
answered grimly enough with André's sentence: 'You could have
been adopted, given the freedom Stretton and I have: to teach
them charity, and you something more about life. And André,
who is infinitely merciful, saw it was no good.'

Paul said, 'Yes, for a Frenchman, he is merciful. But he would
never understand. I think that man below is the devil and that he
is following me.'

The agony in his eyes, blue stones, glazed and burning, convinced Vincent. 'Let's look at it clearly,' he said. 'Why did you
go off with that man?'

'I don't quite know. You see, I'm more accustomed than you
to that sort.'

'Sort of swank then?'

'Perhaps. You've had such luck, you people. I was just as well
raised. And if I'd had your education –'

'Cut that out. If you want education, you'll get it. I'll tell you
this Paul –' The countryman of Blake took a long breath, lifted
the apricot-tanned head, darker than his hair. His eyes counted

paint-flaws on the wall, his imagination aware but sightless. He said: 'That man is an ambulatory, Mediterranean sore, living on the viciousness of our vices. But I think he's a shadow, d'you see – the image, the signature of a very living thing that is your torment. He is nothing, a corpse, a nuisance; but he may be under orders. Orders he knows even.'

Paul amazed him, breaking into sobs, the unfathomable hysteria of the damned. He took him by the shoulders, almost to his heart, and said: 'You have only to summon your courage. It'll come: and he'll melt.'

But Paul sobbed on, racked noises leaving his body, as a man might spew up formless evil spirits. Vincent hitched him into the crook of his arm, each jerk of the slight shoulders registered against his heart. Was this the beginning of purification? He caressed, careful not to talk. Paul at last lay still; then sat up suddenly, slung his fine ankles to the floor, went to the *lavabo* and washed his face with hot water, with cold, with cologne. Drew a wet comb through his hair, worked on his cheeks with a powder-wad.

'Thank you for letting me cry. It did me a lot of good.'

'Where are you going now?'

'Down to the lounge. I don't think he'll come there. I've got a book.'

'What sort of a book?'

'I like it. It is about the sort of gentlemen my people were; like yours. The sort I might have been.' Vincent was conscious of the whine, the sniff, mixed with the utter truth. He sat on the side of the bed, pensive and fatigued.

He went down to the garage and saw to his car; and there, among its intricacies, anchored himself against flights on to planes of suffering which produced the phenomena of one fair boy weeping on his bed, and one green, gap-toothed figure dodging on the quays. Also distaste, division, and disgust among a band of friends. He ate up his car's insides like cake; here was something precise to *do*, for people who were dependants on his car's flights for pleasure. He had worked himself into a serenity, a little too ardent to be sane, when, rising from his knees, he saw the Pimp, looking in at the garage door, pulling something out of his loose pocket, a book or a box.

'Get out!' he cried. The man's mouth moved; it sounded like

whistling. Something flapped. He went off. Up the moonlight-stair Vincent had watched on the last night.

He left the garage and crossed the square to the hotel. It was getting late. In a corner of the empty salon he found Paul with his book. A child sent to Coventry, in the arid, frivolous, depressing room, his face was still scorched with crying.

'Vincent, for pity's sake, don't give me up. It is true what you said; there are evil spirits around me. I've been too kicked to fight them alone. You invited me out of hell into heaven, and it seems I brought my own hell with me. For pity's sake —'

And pity like a naked, new-born babe striding the blast. Vincent flung himself off down the corridor to André's room, and found him alone. 'André, I've sent that child sky-high, and it seems to have kicked him permanently off his legs. I'm out of power; I can't handle him.'

The passionate sentences, thrust into literal French, intrigued André: 'Oh these little boys with more sensibility than wits! I know them. Send him up to me.'

He went back. 'André says you're to go to him.'

'I'm ashamed.'

'Do as he tells you.'

'I'll try.'

Vincent sat on the foot of André's bed. All lights were out but the reading-lamp that lit the Frenchman's hands, the gay, dark, imagination-worn head in rose-gold shadows. Paul drew up a stool to the bed and sat between them, leaning against it, his hands on the sheets.

'*Mon gosse*, what is this trouble about? Vincent tells me that you are afraid of the Pimp. But Stretton says that he saw you talking to him last night.'

'I did worse than that. I went with him up to the old town, with the sailors. Today I saw him again. He would speak to me. Today I saw that there were evil things all round me. And I see the man everywhere. In places where I know he can't be. He is a devil. I am being punished again. I am always being punished —'

André scribbled a note and gave it to Vincent. 'Take that down to the "patron". It is to say that if that man is seen round the hotel again I and my friends leave. That should settle it. Will that do, boy?'

When Vincent returned to his place Paul had drawn closer to the bed, and André's hands were invisible, the boy's face laid on them.

'My little one, you are young and handsome. Clever at some things, Vincent says, and neither poor nor sick. What is it that spoils your life?'

Paul answered in a low voice: 'It has always been the same, André. When I was at school. People were unjust to me. I hadn't laughed much in years till I knew Vincent. He can make me giggle. And in spite of his friends, who hate me, he brought me here and introduced me to you. And my filth's followed me just the same. I'm in prison like I was before. Then something that separates me from you. Dudley and Stretton are quite justified. I shall never hold it against them that they won't know me. But I'm sorry I was rude to you today.'

'It isn't that,' said André, looking out as Vincent had done, summoning his angel. 'It is your attitude to life, to people, that is wrong. Don't you know that the kind of general insolence in which you take pleasure makes people your enemies – separates you, as you say? When your charm is all you have, you ruin it, and wonder that you are ruined. If you used it, you would have friends, and your devils would vanish, and your life fill with pleasantness."

'But I am better, much better, much more moral since Vincent –'

'When did Vincent preach morals to you? Morals are an excuse for a boy of your sort, to justify your tempers. Or hags to ride you to hell. Leave your little virtues alone, and attend to the virtue which gave you Vincent. Don't you know that God does not like us for the things we think good. For the rest, courage –' He pulled a silver ring down his arm and slipped it on the boy's wrist. 'Wear that tonight if you're afraid.' The lovely, tired voice ran on, with passion fatigue seemed to strengthen, and all the vicissitudes of man. Paul kept his face laid on the hand he clung to, the bracelet that had changed wrists lighting the sheets. 'Remember the old woman who had been pious, at heaven's gate, who was secretly afraid because when she was a child she had stolen cherries from a tree. She told Peter all the good she had done, and while he called up God the Father, prayed that the cherry-tree had been forgotten. Until God answered, "Let her in. After all, it's the woman who robbed the cherry-tree." It is a sin to wear thorns when God meant you to wear roses.'

Vincent, silent, curled-up, heard Paul's rare short, flute laugh. Knew he was listening to the Kourotrophos, the bringer-up of boys, André, the peacock of the world, who had borne the cross. Paul was smiling at him, and now he had lifted his head, Vincent saw André's hand wet with tears.

It was late. It seemed as if there was a huge balance in this room, a scale filling up and up against the other which had been filled. Paul's face was hidden again, this time on his knees. André spoke on; but Vincent dreamed that the scales held the life and death of Paul. If the high one sank, a cup would sail in down a light ray (he imagined it through a hole in the shutter slats). There would be a lance with it and an aureole for the boy. If it did not, well, he could only see a seedy man with green teeth following them about.

There was a knock at the door. Without waiting Stretton came in and stood for a moment against André's bath-robes. André said: 'A moment, Stretton.'

Paul sat up, but both he and Vincent had time to see Stretton's face, set like the Lucifer of the English imagination, in blasting pride and contempt. A son of the morning, visiting a son of the morning, his eyes were on Paul, the scorn in them a thing to cross dreams.

André said: 'Come back in a quarter of an hour.' He went out. The high scale stayed in air.

Paul got up. 'Thank you very much, André. You've done me a lot of good. I'll say good night now. I'm very tired. Good night.'

Vincent followed him. 'Well,' he said, 'now can you have a little faith?' and saw Paul look at him with lost sweetness that hardened again through misery past comprehension to a coarse denial that would never leave him again.

'Almost,' he said, 'I had. It was like music that you could see. Till Stretton knocked. Then it turned not real, flat, a bit of pretence. Stretton did it. He meant it too. He's in with the man on the quays.' And at Vincent's agonized laugh: 'I'm not so frightened now. I reckon I can get along. But not as André meant. Or you. Not after the way Stretton looked at me. He's put me back in my place. I know now that the filthy can never mix with the clean.

He won't forgive you in a hurry either. Or André, when he's thought it over. D'you think I need give him back his bracelet? The boys in Paris will make a fine story out of it. Sorry, Vincent. I hope, I hope – Oh, only that Stretton will never be able to bitch you as he's bitched me.'

Vincent felt very cold – utterly tired. He took Paul's wrist and slipped off André's silver ring. 'If you ever want it back, you will only have to ask for it.'

'Thanks, but I shan't. I'm off tomorrow. Run in to you some-time if you care to remember me. I should like that – Vincent, you're a poor fish to take it so hard. It's my business. I shall be gone before the rest of you are up. Good night.'

Angele au Couvent

I

Their school was built inside the ruins of a monastery on the coast of Fife. The playing fields were enclosed with huge walls. Among them were a few garden-plots and a thin line of trees. On one side of the wall the sea went roaring night and day. At the intersection of the walls there was sometimes a tower. One was a pigeon-tower, full of holes. The trees, that were a row of whistles for the wind, grew small out of the bright grass. Outside the wall there was a ruin and a saint's tower. The school-tower, ill-proportioned and built of the same stone, overlooked the square. There was never anything but wind in the town whose pride was to grow in spite of nature and also to outdo nature and laugh at nature.

The girls went about the country in solitary couples, trudging, chatting. At night they were shut up under the towers, inside the walls. Those who loved the school rarely went outside. They were girl-athletes, running like deer inside the walls, leaping, turning, charging in a group, scattering to reassemble, passing slowly, cowled like young monks, into lit, stone houses at dusk. They were young monks, vowed to obedience, labour, chastely ignorant of chastity, rewarded by authority and power. The model was a god-centred word, and sometime the god had been lost, and his place taken by rules and ranks, and by great cold, and at night by the voices of the sea.

They were girls grown as boys and turned, occasionally, into animals who had lost their sex. There was to be found in them a cynicism and a true accidia that they sweated out running in the wind.

47

A girl walked on a path cut off from the wind, under young lime-trees, on soaked gravel. The sun splintered on the top of the wall, bright, cold gold. It would soon rain-in the March night.

She pulled on her hood lined with bright silk and enjoyed its touch, and out of her serge tunic pocket, over one small breast, took out a rosary she had made of nutmegs and peach-stones, spaced with red beans and finished with a cross. She was taught that it was wrong to pray to the Virgin, so it might be true. 'Hail, Mary,' she said, also the *sursum corda* and a psalm of penitence, going from bead to bead till she had had enough of it and there were seven beads left. She tried to make up a prayer. The sun had sunk behind the wall into wet, gold air. At supper, because it was Saturday, there would be richer food. She paced back, her eyes watching inside her hood, contemplative, up-and-sideways-looking, underscored with blue on a milky skin. Her head went up, safe inside her hood she was all attention, calling to any daimon to come and play, at anything, in a darkening garden, in Scotland, at the beginning of night.

God is a spirit. The cold wind rose.

God is the helping of man by man. Who helps me with my algebra? A mouse ran across her path, a gull cried over her.

God is a gentleman. No, that's the devil. The devil's a part of God. I always thought that myself. Lord, give me something to play with. Make my Cicero translate right. Forgive the devil and comfort him. Let Doris be my friend. Make tomorrow all right. I must finish my beads. A poem will do. She went on and looking at the dark grass said, *Round the stem of the Fairy Tree.*

A house-mistress with a lantern overtook her.

'Are you out so early from Confirmation Class?'

'I do not go, Miss Mackail; I have been confirmed.'

'I see.' She went on. The girl stepped out into the dark and trudged in her round snow-boots after the swinging light circle, and the powerful idol travelling on its edge. She wanted her to be a jolly old lady, who would call her and give her buttered toast and ask her what she thought about life. There was supposed to be a house-mistress who did that, who let her girls stay over when they had colds.

The night arrived. The clock-tower struck half-past six. The old tower sank into the night's iron sky. Her head was cooled and rested from the schoolroom's noise. Her colt's legs ached. Dry wires of hair rubbed her forehead under her hood.

In the schoolroom, on her desk, she found her sewing returned for the blood-stitched buttons to be taken off and put on again. The spread of calico had knocked over her flowers. 'That woman's a beast,' she said, and put a head of cotton through a darning-needle and tied the ends. The child's infinite capacity for leisure was being introduced to another kind of time, full of ends and beginnings and things which had to be done.

The Saturday night crowd, rested and expansive, saw her.

'Crazy Terry in from the playground so early,' they sang and jerked the back of her chair.

Her only chance was to amuse them, to be a little crazy. A small, chlorotic matron interrupted them to say that her sewing was disgraceful. She sucked a finger rough with threads of skin.....

'That's right,' said a girl, 'go on. You like being called Crazy Terry because you think you're different. But you aren't. You're just like everyone else. Ruth's going to give you a prefect's jaw about trying to be different.' The tribal life whooped off.

'Silence,' called a prefect.

'Why?' said a girl who knew a great many boys and wore her hair all the holidays in a white ribbon, and lived near London, in a large red house and grounds and went up to London in a car.

'Fifty lines by tomorrow morning to anyone who speaks again.'

In the silence the cold could be felt passing in at every window of the long room. Terry noticed that the low sky looked as if it were dark blue and was glad to be quiet.

'It's because of the people who're going to be confirmed,' whispered the girl and put out her tongue.

The new kind of time stopped. Terry had ruled off the end of her Latin dictionary into squares which were the days of the term, and she now had a square to fill in with a design for the kind of day it had been. The day before had a crescent inside a smaller square, which meant the new moon seen through glass, and accounted for the return of the buttons. A coarse darner makes a large hole in a linen button. She looked through it at a piece of the room. The gas whistled in the hazy air.

I saw a tree with gold fruit. It didn't mean anything. I was top in English, that's a Solomon's Seal. If I score off Rachel I'll draw a swastika on Monday because she's a Jewess.

She practised swastikas and counted up the days to the term's end.

There was a girl who had asked Terry to explain the Faerie Queen. She had interesting square bones and a blonde skin that tanned. Terry with dark spiral curls admired her, but she belonged to another girl, the daughter of an Indian Colonel, whose life was on a pert convention. Terry did not understand. She had thought until lately that there was a god who gave things it was good for people to have. She had asked him for Doris. There had been delicious scraps. She understood she was no match for the girl who had Doris, but did not understand why.

The Sunday was brilliantly cold. At the end of the afternoon walk their shins were sore through their wool stockings. The schoolroom fire roared. The prefects had tea in the house-mistress's warm drawing-room. Time, that all the week hummed like a taut rope, moved into a slow beat, and Terry, at her ease, made her own time.

Doris and her friend had been confirmed the night before. Unexpectedly Doris came over to her and said:

'Will you come out into the playground, Terry? I want to talk... You can't come out like that. Go and get a sweater or something.'

Terry ran, and at the foot of the stairs stood still, glowing and in pain that there should be someone to tell her to put on a sweater when it was so cold.

In the Blue Dormitory Doris's friend was in her cubicle as Terry passed, putting up a sickly head of Christ, by Dolci, on the wall.

Terry knew that that sort of picture was not a good picture. It did not help her at all to think of a man like that. Old maids like him and people called Pale Virgins in the old song. The child did not identify herself and correctly. She intended that Doris should not think like that.

The girl saw her.

'Do you like my picture, Terry Vane?'

'Well, not very much. Stiff plain Christs I like better.'

She was busy giving the girl a sensibility equal to her own.

'I don't suppose you would see what's in it,' said the girl, who was overwrought and whom Doris had told that Terry had a wonderful mind and whom a little daring would have sent whimpering to another friend.

Then Terry would have been protected and Doris sensitized, but Terry thinking only of the playground, ran away from her into her cubicle and snatched a sweater and with her cloak unfastened, walked her friend out and away.

Doris unhooded her bold, intelligent head. Terry seldom wore her hood because, as the house suspected, she loved her own hair. They shook off other strollers and reached a wide drive that commanded the sea.

'Well?' said the child.

'Look here, Terry, for three weeks I've been to the parson's lectures and all I remember is that there was a council at Nicaea where somebody decided that the Son was one substance with the Father. There's one thing, and what has it to do with my duty to my neighbours and what have either of them to do with eating bread and wine in church? I was so nervous this morning I might have been sick. My sister used to have tea and a biscuit before she went, but she doesn't go now. What is one to believe? Or do, once one believes?'

Terry said: 'We can chuck the council of Nicaea, anyhow.'

'Then the catechism?'

'That's just how people would like us to believe.'

Doris grinned.

'But, Terry, who cares if we believe? That's what I want to know. Is there a God at all that we've any reliable information about? I mean is the Bible true? There's something called the higher criticism that says the Bible didn't happen.'

'My bishop talked about that and told us to ignore it. So I asked. It's about the flood. All those animals couldn't have got into the ark.'

The blue-pearl-coloured sea hammered on the reefs that are the coast of Fife. *Black rock and skerry* ravelling the pure water that comes from the pole into a mantling for the sea. The bitter air was cold gold, the smoke of the Scots town enchanted it. A star came out. Terry looked at it and a white ivy leaf on the wall and at the texture of old stone. The sky was green in the South. She smiled, passing into those beauties.

'What would God say, Terry, to my brother? He likes horses and he drinks, and knows about life, and when he comes into the room it goes with a swing and father's friends look small, and father gets mad and Dick just laughs. On all accounts Dick's damned. But if God isn't decent to Dick –'

'God's got to be –'

'Well, if the parson's God isn't true, is there anything? Muriel says it's Christ that matters. I can't see there's anything so wonderful there. Would you mind a few years' bad time if you knew you were going to be taken off directly it was over by millions of angels to have a good time for ever. Besides, He was never married and books are about being in love.'

'Her picture is awful.'

'Good for you, Terry. She got mad when I didn't like it. Now you've said so.'

Terry's cheek was like milk and wine.

'Doris, I know there is a God. But the point about God is that parsons and churches spoil Him. He exists only when you are by yourself and see that things are beautiful.'

'Yes,' said Doris, 'go on.'

'He writes His name everywhere for us to see. Look at those purple cabbages. Think of an ice. That's God being friendly. Like your brother's horses. They said Christ ate and drank.'

'Never too much, Terry.'

'Wine and things He liked, if He was God at all.'

'Wasn't He God? You don't think He was God?'

More stars came out. Terry saw a feather-moon turn into a gold knife. They were out in the centre of a great playing-field. The whole sky was over them. She put up her face for it to kiss.

'No. I understand. It is not a man or a woman. It's more like the bird they call the Holy Ghost.'

'It is every beautiful thing.

'It is the stars coming out and the orange square of those windows. Where we must go back.

'It is every good thing.

'It is especially love.

'It is us when we see it. We are God.

'There, that is all I know. Will that do?'

'I am going to try and believe it. Oh, Terry, you've said everything.'

'Remember, if it isn't true, we've got to go to hell with the people who wanted it to be true.'

'Heaven for climate, hell for company. I'm with you, Terry.'

Terry thought: Will she stay with me now?

Across the brightness of her suddenly simplified conception, the question wrote itself in black. She was breathless with pleasure, but she understood that the answer was not yes.

'Still thinking, Terry?'

'Yes.'

'Well?'

'Only that what I have seen is good enough. I mean that it is all that I shall have.'

Doris looked aside.

'It seems to me that you have everything. Do you mind if we go back. I promised Muriel to make toast and go through tomorrow's prose.'

'Will you go through my prose, too?'

'Yes, if there's time.'

And Muriel does not mind, – Terry thought and had not the courage to say, and this understanding lay, like a bitter almond she would afterwards learn to appreciate, in the honey of the child's mind.

II

A girl blew a whistle. On a remote playing field they put on their cloaks and sorted out, two and two, to return. Terry under a tree saw them coming and turned back over squeaking wet turf. The even rollers of the sea ran up the beaches. She looked to see if the sun had coloured them. There were birds in the gold air behind the leaves whose turnings made her sick, and no colour in the grey water she could hear all day and all night, except when she was in school.

She imagined that she was ill and would not go over to school, but sit out there all night under a small tree and watch the uncoloured sea till it could only be heard. She was afraid of the people of the place. She was not ill and they would find her, they would ask her questions and punish her. It did not occur to her that they could be right in anything they did, or that she could defy them. She ignored them because she could not do anything else but – she was at their mercy and in fear. The wind was cold, the ground was wet – she went in at the tail of the cloaked girls.

'Where have you been, Terry? Mooning about the courts. We saw you.'

'Who cares if you did?'

Anyone could see I care. God how I hate them.

In half-an-hour there would be the hour's preparation, food, then another hour's work, then bed in the icy whistling dormitories. She did not understand the work. She did not always listen when they explained. They said she could do it if she liked. This morning she had not listened. She had forgotten to attend to the beginning and there was no one who would tell her. There was a lesson to be done about Hebrew prophets. 'One hour a week at that and five at algebra,' she said, and drank a mug of weak tea. The tiny stimulus acted. In the hall she hung about and looked at the curve of the old stairs.

The house-mistress came out of her room. 'Isn't it time you went over to school?'

'Not for five minutes,' said Terry simply, and went away. She did not know that the sight of her, all sizes and none adjusted, exasperated the athletic woman.

'She is not wholesome,' she said, and thought of the splendid machine she captained, also of the kind of girl she liked, neat, sturdy, predictable, smart. These were her pride. There was her technique.

Terry went back and drank some tea from the bottom of the pot. She began to see night coming, light ebbing and replaced by light. Between their pools she could be lost. She threw a Spenser into her satchel and ran across into school.

High up there was a varnished hall where the lower school did its preparation. From the roof, enormous lights threw a just-sufficient glow on to the desks. On the platform one of the sixth form kept the room, doing her almost grown-up work, writing with a fountain-pen. From time to time a girl left her place, walked up the steps, asked permission from her and went away. That was all that would happen for two hours. Terry would not have to go away. She slid sideways into her seat, curled down and looked about her. The tea worked. She thought of the fast waters of the burn bubbling, and of a girl she admired and had seen throwing up a ball and jumping to meet it and of her beautiful legs. That she was called clumsy Terry and that she could describe what they did and that it did not count. 'Writing is my only joy,' and that was like a song. Songs were literature. She could do literature better than them all. She knew things in a flash, out of nowhere. She spoke when no one else could. There was silence and she felt warm for days. But it was not possible to trade the flesh with the grown-up women for the algebra and the arithmetic. They would only be paid in their own coin and she could not earn it. Not if all day and through her sleep she tried to find their pennies. She could not pay them. She did not know what they wanted. The others all spoke together, 'Yes, yes,' they said and handed in clean competent pages and grumbled for swank. She never pretended not to understand a lesson when she did. Oh, yes, I do unless they call me conceited. On the days I can't stand them I pretend not to understand. The things they can do they won't help me with. No one ever told me how they began, why you have to take a and b away from each other. Mother says she had no education, and if I make such a fuss about it, I can look out for myself. Mother is not like the mothers in books.

She did her algebra wrong, and comforted herself preparing a poem, satisfied her sense of justice, quieted her fear of the next day. She got word and sense perfect, she rested, she lived, she began to be hungry.

Next day the algebra was returned to her to be done again, alone, that afternoon, when the others were out in the fields, the headmistress to be told, the house-mistress, the captain of the house. Terry could not see. Sweat broke out of the milk-bright skin, on to the rough wood. Cold followed sweat. Lead crept in her veins. Before her the heavy disgusted face of the mistress sucked the corners of its mouth. Horrible tears rushed up her and were held, bolted back by her teeth. *They shall not pass the barrier of my teeth.* She went into the literature class, where now her back was broken she could still speak. She knew it all, and she could not make a mistake; she was praised. It counted for nothing. Like quiet it half restored her. Like a little cup of wine it heartened her for something that she could not bear. Her isolation among the insatiable women became a state she had entered.

She reported after school to the headmistress and was contemptuously dismissed. 'You here again, Terry Vane.' It banged in her head, a dance-step trodden by great beasts. She was all small in a wood. A baby terror woke.

Hark, hark,
The dogs do bark,
The beggars are coming to town.

Enemies were singing towards her. She went over to the house, too sick to eat.

After lunch she had to sit and sew. The other girls had seen her outside the headmistress's door. She wanted them to say things. A prefect whispered to another, and a girl she did not like joined them.

Her house-mistress was more explicit. 'I wish you to understand, Terry, that your conduct is disgraceful. It is utterly unsatisfactory. Until I have evidence of improvement I shall recommend that you do no more literature.'

At first she could have stunned herself with crying; wailing, imploring, have dropped before the woman. She had not the courage of abandon. She looked stupidly out of the window, lived a long time, forgot.

She was outside. 'Devils,' said the child. 'Devils. No God.' She thought of God as quite helpless too, and went clumsily downstairs.

'I'm sorry, Ruth, I can't play till half-time, I have to go to a detention.'

'Really, Terry, I call that carrying slackness rather far. You won't work and you won't play except at things you think you are good at.'

A monster that would not work and would not play formed in her mind. She remembered that at night it was dark. Then her mind ran out into a place where people were free and pranced along with grapes in their hair. It was either silly, or too good to be true. She wanted to be out and moving in the cold. In the passage they were fighting to be ready for play. She took her books and went back again into school.

Now it was empty, the great skeleton house that rushed with life and murmured with classes, quite empty. She could not hide in it. One or two others, also sent back, passed her without speaking. She could have smiled, but thought they despised her and acquiesced. She thought of an impudent game they might have played before the mistress came, and imagined it played, went into an empty class-room, opened a clean page and waited.

No one came. She was cold. She had been six terms in the place. The end would be in two years. She had been driven up north. She had only asked to be taught like a boy. She would go back south, from one failure to another, into dusty gold out of grey wind.

'I did not think I could not do anything. They are making me so that I can't do anything at all.' A band outside began,

O ye take the high road
And I'll take the low road
And I'll be in Scotland afore ye.

The tune rose in her head, it was good to be alone, high up in a room all windows, and hear music. She began to walk about, singing quietly, not in tune, swinging her curls. She warmed, tune followed tune. The mistress, coming along the passage, saw her through the glass door, saw her come back again and again to the window, and sit on it, looking down into the town and up into the sky.

'I told you to wait for me in B. This is D.'

'I'm sorry, Miss Keith, I thought you said in here.'

'Your work is disgraceful. I don't know what to do with you. You have ability.'

The tune had drawn the child into a pattern. Terry said: 'I can do one thing well. I can understand the value of words and quantities. The words in this stuff are just made up. It doesn't interest me. It might –'

The woman was astonished into attention. 'It might if what –?'

The music stopped. Terry looked round the dull walls.

'I don't know. It doesn't matter.' If I could tell the woman. If I could ask her to explain from the beginning. It isn't worth it. She wouldn't. They like to bully. I can't say it. I must get it over. I must get away. She saw herself running, first against the woman

beating her with her hands, then past her crying till the need for
steady breath stopped her, and she was out of the place, out and
out on the Fifeshire roads, till she met a man on a horse, who
picked her up. She wondered how long she had taken thinking.
She opened the textbook.

'It was seven and eight I got wrong.'

'I set from six to ten.'

'I got six right.'

'I returned your work for gross inaccuracy in the eighth example.'

The man was with Terry, waiting for her at the class-room
door. She shrugged her shoulders.

'Show me what I did wrong, please.'

'Terry, that is not the way to speak.'

She sighed into herself. The woman looked at her. She was
white and she had been red. She showed her exactly what she
had done.

'Don't let it happen again. I am sure you could do better work
if you liked.'

Better. She could do it perfectly or not at all. She withdrew
herself. The band began again. *Turn ye to me* it played, and a
point was touched to bliss like sexual pleasure in a little star.
Never listen to anything but that sound. 'May I stay a moment?'
she said cunningly. 'I should like to go through it again while I
remember to understand.' The pretty appeal worked. Pleased,
she put out her tongue as the mistress went through the door,
and sat behind her desk listening.

The tune was new. She waited for the repeats and sucked them
in. 'Ai, ai,' she sighed in exquisite desolation.

She remembered that she was not to be allowed to learn literature any more. There would not be a band every day. Bands
were not verses. Her nerves, plucked by the music, resolved into
active passion. She was strong and went into agony. She leapt up
and ran, down the stairs, into the playground. Scotch mist was
brimming the air softly. Balls were clicking through it, all the
school was playing. She could not be alone. She did not want the
old kind man on the horse.

'*Turn ye to me*, it's called. *Turn ye to me*,' she said to the great
wall. A bird flew out of it and the haar curled. '*Turn ye to me*,'

she said evoking the girls of the house and gave a little shriek of
pain walking up and down, up and down the cinder track,
drenched and wild. The rain increased. There were hooded
figures coming up the path. She turned back, the rain driving
through her coarse stockings. She ran up to her cubicle. In the
old green passage the lights were lit. She was afraid of colds and
tore off her stockings and tunic, put on a white frock and her
evening shoes.

'Turn to me. Oh, something turn to me. There is nothing. If
I am not to learn literature I shall die.'

'Die,' said the wind rising out of the inaudible sea. In the
dormitories the white enamelled walls glittered like ice. The old,
green passage had deep windows. She sprang on to a sill and
played that she was lying in the arms of the sea.

The tune ebbed in her brain. She noticed that it was not so
important now if she did not learn literature. She could teach
herself. She could not help learning it. She would certainly learn
nothing else. The deprivation was a mask, the house-mistress
pushed up to be a paste-board cow for the enemy that would
stalk her all her life. The enemy moved in every person. It was
not a person but a reaction in persons from her yet uncrystallized
sensibility.

'*Look out, my lovely one.*' A charming young man was speaking
to her. Nicer than the old man on the horse.

'*Good luck to you,*' he said and vanished. She sighed and came
to herself.

'God is a beast. Perhaps He is miserable like me.'

She thought that the young man on the screen of her imagination was sad. A girl passed her, a stock-broker's daughter, with
leering eyes and a rich frock.

'I suppose you're ashamed to go down.'

'No.'

'Well, I should have some tea if I was you and get it over.'

'Thanks.'

That's June. Insult one and pat. I must have something that
lasts in this world.

She went downstairs and found that she could not pass the
schoolroom door. She remembered scented woods by the sea.
The house-mistress called down the bannisters.

'I wonder if you would go over to school and fetch me my purse? I left it on the table in the mistress's room.'

Terry heard the drawing-room door shut. As if nothing had happened. It was their bluff to pretend to mind what one did. She went out by the forbidden front door, across the quadrangle, running delicately in her thin shoes. She was going somewhere interesting. In the mistress's room there might be curious things that explained what went on there and the secret ideas that govern the regiment of women. Half-way up the stairs she felt very tired. The place was enormous now it was dark. She had heard of a ghost. She hurried, sighed and cooled her forehead against the door. She knocked. There was no answer. She went in, saw a bead of gas in the dusk, pulled the little chain, saw the purse and looked round. The room was full of shabby papers, but there was a fire and a deep empty chair. She lay down on it. There was nothing interesting. Only a re-statement of some of the poorer girls grown up. The chair only was good, and the fire. She wanted to lie there the rest of the day, in the heart of the enemies' country, be found lounging in a chair. It was like playing Indians.

She could not move. She must not. She must not rest. She thought of the school getting darker, that would not be filled for an hour.

The men were lighting up the place into a blaze. She did not remember. She lay before the rich fire. She saw the purse on the table, struggled up and fell back. Then she forgot what she was doing.

She saw a young man on the wall. He was Hermes with a child on his arm. She had gone out of life and he was taking notice of her.

She saw that it was a large print of a statue, unwound off a roller, and hung on a wall and she began to remember who Hermes was.

That's a great statue. That's beautiful. I suppose men's bodies are like that.

Oh, the old woman's purse.

She dropped off the wheel of her environment and saw the feelings of the day in a pattern unrelated to the pain of her small pains. They interested her, and there passed into her curiosity, elation, power. She saw the image of Hermes and that it was outside the time in which she was living and the people to whom she was subject, and that through her pleasure in him, she could live in his time and turn round in it and come out again. The old woman wanted her purse.

I shall see things in the world where Hermes is, and when I come out these people will leave me alone.

She chewed on the prospect of alarming the mistresses. She annihilated the years to her maturity and remembered them.

Divine Hermes, don't let me forget you. The old woman wants her purse.

Hermes, Hermes, before I saw you here, you were the boy who came and talked to me this afternoon instead of the old man.

I must take the old woman her purse.

The Later Life of Theseus, King of Athens
(From the *Memoirs of Menestheus, the Erechthid*)

We were all without illusion that any good was to be expected from these affairs. From the first they appeared deplorable; now that the worst has happened, I can only repeat that it was expected, foreseen, foretold; and that, as so often occurs, now it is over, the situation is left much as it was before.

Now that the government in Athens has changed, as it was bound to change, it can be seen that the activities of the late king were no more than the wind ruffling the unstirred baths of ocean. Wherein exist those dumb and flexible powers who reigned before him, and have been shown to survive him. I mean that I, after these years of exile and observation, have come back into my place. Or, it would be more prudent and more cautious to say, that a place has come back and been filled by me.

Theseus has gone. He was not legitimate. Not one of those earth-sprung princes created to rule because, in some sense, he *is* this piece of earth. He had no business here in Athens at all, though he might have done well enough in Trozên. When he chose to come and lord it here, he should not have been surprised if, though the people applauded him, the air and the stones did not accept him; and that in time the people of this ancient situation were repersuaded, not by him, but by the stones and the air.

Theseus went. During his reign I watched his efforts. I and others, and knew that all we had to do was wait and watch the spending of his energy, and even admire its furious turns. It passed. When it was over, I returned and took my place. The land sighed, turned over, and now sleeps again.

But what a time we had! New laws, new drains, new wives.

I remember as if it were yesterday the morning that Phædra arrived in her Cretan ship. The daughter of Minos and of Pasiphæ, she seemed a staring, silly maid. A little subnormal, I thought, a freak of over-breeding. She was very quiet in the palace, though I was rather pleased at the shrine she built to a featureless, but peculiar, Aphrodite.

There is nothing I deplore more than the effort made by men like Theseus to abstract and beautify the Gods. At the same time to make them into men. I and my friends know that they are neither abstract, human, nor necessarily beautiful. So I welcomed the gesture of Theseus' wife; but, again, I may have idealized it. She was probably homesick for some uncertain Cretan daimon, a furtive goddess-of-woman-indoors.

Well, the Cretan neurosis soon found its expression. As is usual in these affairs, it was the talk of the place before the actors and sufferers were aware of their own passion.

What no one foresaw was the appeal to Poseidon. Nor the immediate response, in circumstances when a god such as Theseus conceived, might well have counted seven. In half an hour the matter would have been explained. Artemis should have seen to that. Personally, I wish Poseidon had let Hippolytos be, promise or no promise. Only I knew that the divine element must always work like that. It is an automatic quality, and the Gods, when they act, are so much stored power released. In the same manner, Artemis did not come until Hippolytos' extremity compelled her. A racing Goddess, but a woman!

But it is entirely inopportune to speculate on what ought to have happened. Theseus, our late showman, gave us an exhibition that will not soon be forgotten. It was not the first. It proved not to be the last.

In the first months of his widowhood, his energy in passing new laws is impossible to describe. It became difficult, before the feast of Anthesteria, to catch sprats: to draw water between sunset and midnight from the public fountains. And forbidden to invoke Poseidon on any account at all.

It became impossible to marry one's aunt; and there were regulations as to the destruction of fish-heads in hot weather, for which I think there is something to be said. At the same time, the war he made almost immediately on the Lapiths was plain evidence that his character was weakening.

We did not oppose it. There are worse things than a small war, fought in one's own place, so as not to interfere with the harvest. I was not curious about the Lapiths, but when a community is ruled by a man like Theseus, kept in a constant state of excitement, with nothing to do but neglect its business to talk, not even about his ideas, but about him, I considered that their arrival was reasonably well timed.

Personally, I believe he invited them, but I will describe, as I saw it, the result of the first and only battle in the campaign.

Indeed, it is well known how they met, Theseus and that old scoundrel Perithoös. How they craned over their chariots to observe each other and Theseus countermanded the charge; and how they walked out between the lines and examined one another until Theseus kissed him.

The city knows how they came back, arm in arm, both sides straggling behind them; and the noise they made opening up the palace for the foreign army to get at the wine. It had always been more of an inn than a gentleman's residence. The little Queen Phædra tried to introduce Cretan formality. Theseus had played at that, but not for long. There was no ceremony that night, when they roared their songs and rang their cups, and lit cressets, whose light danced in the wind on the marble and lit the palace right out to sea.

At dawn they went roaring down to the Piræus, and I thought of the wonderful luck of the man, to whom the next event was always kind. There is a kind of compensation for the man who uses life, who gets into trouble and into pleasure as a boat runs from tack to tack. He had better remember though that he is used, and not so honourably, as the man who submits to life's using of him. I might have been a Theseus.

But there they were that night, Theseus and Perithoös, the heroes. He sent his Lapiths home, but he stayed; and they went riding together, went drinking, went talking, until the town began to say: 'The end of this will be a new Queen.'

It must be remembered that he was not a man to act upon design, and one who would as lightly have offended the Dioscuri as he would have taken Heracles into his own house, when that hero had gone mad and murdered his own children. The fool never knew that blood will do more than out; that blood will have blood. He has been praised for what he did then, for his friendship with a man so close to him in temperament that he could despise his madness and the pollution of his blood; keeping him with him till his wits came back, and telling him that the sole evil in his act was his terror of it.

I heard that said, and saw Heracles comforted at last. I smiled. I do not know what blood is, but it is not so easily got rid of. The earth wins at last. We shall go down to the house of Hades, and there will be no more of those swaggering Olympians, and the heroes they have so jovially begot. And I mean to be on the side that must win, if it means a lifetime of quiet.

Besides, I saw Perithoös chewing a twig of buckthorn last March; for a purge, I suppose, not uneasiness – before they began the scandalous entertainment we witnessed when they stole the immortal sister of the Dioscuri, Helen-of-the-Egg, the daughter of Leda and the Swan.

I do not doubt that people were right when they said that the suggestion came from Perithoös. He would have done anything for Theseus, who, I suppose, said something like this: 'Those neurotic Cretan sisters were both a mistake. One to hang herself, the other to go off with a god. Hippolyta was too much the other way. We were too alike; I was unfair to her, and I'm sorry for it now. I did not treat her as I would have been treated, and it is a shame to me. There are only Phædra's children left; I don't like the breed. I must have another choice of heirs; and a fine Greek, this time, Perithoös.'

Then Perithoös suggested, without an idea but to get his friend what he wanted: 'Why not a goddess this time, Theseus?'

I suppose they discussed it a little, but I am sure that after a hundred words they were asking: 'Which one?' And when I consider their difficulties, I do not wholly reject their choice.

Every far-seeing and observant man has had his eye on the nursery of King Tyndareus. The girls were born to be queens in Hellas. Queens have come to no good lately in this city, but there was no harm in Theseus asking. Only, when he asked for her, he was refused on the count that she was a child.

The reason was not only sufficient, it was true. But Theseus and Perithoös left the city at once. A month later they came back arm in arm and told the town they had stolen her.

To marry her? No! For ransom? Not at all. But to live with his mother for three years till she should be old enough for marriage. Anyone could see that this would not do. What did he suppose her brothers would have to say about it? The Dioscuri are a notable pair of young men. Far better to have married her at once, child or no child; but that is the sort of thing Theseus would not do.

I immediately retired to my country estate, where they would know where to find me.

Theseus made no excuses. I cannot suppose that he had any. He is reported to have said that the marriage would make for peace in Hellas, and one of the Fates would cut her throat when she heard about it; but that he could not touch a child. His position seemed contradictory. I suppose he was vain enough to want her conspicuous beauty. At his age, who had had Ariadne, Phædra, and Hippolyta! I waited with impatience for her brothers, hoping to hear a piece of the divine mind and watch a contest between an old hero and the young. I am not a hero. I and my house were before this fashion for law-givers and deliverers and unfortunate husbands; and I shall be here when some funeral games, getting cheaper every year, are all that is left of them. I should not be surprised if it is we who will insist on some small decencies being preserved, and an offering of at least a minimum of honey and hair. All the same, since ceremonies round holy graves are a part of public life, why not have the body in the grave practically anonymous and the Sacred Snake? It is known what the Sacred Snake is there for. At the same time it is not known. Certainly I would have Theseus forgotten as Theseus.

I will not describe what happened. There was an attempt made to hide the girl. Theseus had brought her to his mother; but this was not generally known. I was looking for her myself, in a strange place, when I came upon the brothers, Castor and Polydeuces, doing the same thing. I offered them my reflections, nothing more. They were too innocent to use and too proud to influence. One is a king's son and the other the son of Zeus; but my position is less equivocal than theirs. Not that they recognized it, blown as they were with these new splendours; but they were boys enough to be glad of any company, and to explain why they were found among the cliffs at Scyros in a cave.

Their objections to the marriage were obscure and mostly untrue. They said that Theseus was too old; which did not matter. They said his former marriages had been unfortunate; which is immaterial. Then they implied that Theseus had foreknowledge, and was deliberately doing what was bound not to happen; which is impossible.

They showed no love for their sister, but an acceptance of her as though she were a part of nature. Not as men speak from pride of race.

They took her away, I was told, in silence. Afterwards Theseus and Perithoös were seen on the terrace, looking out to sea, for a long time, together and also silent.

I did not pretend to understand. The life of the girl Helen has been worth attention. I felt that she was of the same stuff as myself, put to the uses of those new heroes. The uses to which she had put them we are beginning to learn. They have forgotten that there were potencies here before Zeus. But this affair began with a jovial theft of a pretty child and some inconsistent behaviour. It ended with the return of the child, and it was plain to see that Theseus did not think that he had lost one scruple of his dignity.

Knowing that he was soon likely to attempt an even more conspicuous adventure, I had a time of indecision, when I questioned myself, not for the first time, as to what I had gained by the part in life that I had played.

Before the Argo's voyage and the hunt of the Calydonian boar, life moved quietly in this land, arranged on certain antique forms. These I have upheld against the innovating heroes. There are dark spots in nature; let them stay dark. Man need not try to illuminate them. His business is to keep harmony by due propitiatory sacrifices to the infernal powers. I would offend no Sacred Snake. Omit no libation of honey, milk, or blood. Especially not blood. It is, when you think of it, the cheapest of the three.

That there are powers propitious to men I do not deny. That the unpropitious can be disregarded I hold to be the belief of an idiot child, or to deny that man is man's wolf. Hard, pliant, and astute he must be, observant of birds and the prohibitions of his folk.

That is what these men are not doing. In the place of nature they have put their own wills. The Minotaur died, but the Cretan curse returned. I was sorry for Hippolytos, the son of a virago, our hero king made a martyr of.

What has the Golden Fleece done for us? Gold will go back the way it came. I have seen this in the sky.

With three queens under the earth and one refused him, with heirs of kind to succeed him, the ruler of a people who cheered him and twittered at him, but who were really waiting for me; in the late middle years of his life, Theseus decided that he had not dared enough, and that the time had come for a yet more outrageous enterprise. He had lost the young Helen. Well and good! This time he would have a goddess.

It was said that Pallas Athene was his first choice. I wondered mildly what she would have thought of Phædra's small white palace after her Olympian house. Of course I remembered that in earlier days her life had been simple, and she had exacted from us no more tendance than was customary when our lives were simple too. That was before these goddesses had gone up in the world, and all became daft on heroes.

Jealous, also, of each other. Artemis attended Hippolytos' death and swore to Aphrodite that she would kill Adonis for it. That, I suppose, is going on somewhere. But would they allow themselves to be stolen? Anyhow, Theseus changed his mind. He and Perithoös went away, side by side, in two small chariots, and no one knew where they were going. They did not return, and slowly the tale came round that two handsome men of middle age had been seen going down to the house of Death and Persephone. They went through the mountain. They came to the place. They crossed Acheron, Cocytos, Styx; I do not know how they managed Cerberos. To end it, they got inside.

They had come to steal Persephone.

They stole Persephone. I am telling you what happened. I do not know how they did it. Nor what they said to her. It is a long time since she lost her habit of reappearing among us in the spring. Also, there is something about the house of Hades that is agreeable to women. Most of the conspicuous ones there are men, but a woman sits on the throne of that house and distributes its poppies. It is all Persephone, and Eurydice who a man put back. Only, it seems certain that she was willing to go with them. Here on the earth one may guess what will happen, but there may be more chances in the house of Hades. It is a terror to me to admit it, but certainly, since those two went there, the place has also lost much of its prestige. I can no longer see it, half-lit, smelling of dark flowers and blood. I wish I knew how they had persuaded her. Unless he was lying, and Theseus did not lie, she said she would come and live with him in his Athenian house and be a queen to this city. What did they offer her? What did she ask? It happened quickly, I imagine, but she came away between them.

Then Cerberos caught them at the door, and all I heard was that Persephone herself was turned back, and Theseus' bottom stuck to a rock, and of Perithoös nothing was said.

It was then that opportunity found me, and I became king in Athens, and did something to restore old ways and discourage conversation. I was in the full interest of my negative experiments when they returned, first Perithoös, then Theseus.

They seemed to take more pleasure in my society than they had done, and were good enough to say that they found me unchanged. I could not say that of them. They were older. They were fatigued. There is one thing certain about these heroes, that they wear themselves into their graves. And they do not wear well. However, I thought it becoming to give up the kingship at once.

We were back where we had started, nearly a lifetime ago; and time was now our common enemy. If I had realized it then, I should have grieved to have given up that which I had waited for so long. But it had always seemed to me that Theseus was mortal, and I the immortal; for I come of the life that rises and flowers and passes down into the earth again. From uncountable ages my fathers were the earth-kings of this place, and for them the earth's luck held, and they were reborn in their sons for ever. Only I have no son. In me, to the last in direct line, Athens has returned to her kings, seed of the Erecthidæ, sprung of the soil. So I conquered Theseus, the hero who did not understand these things.

I have striven to alter nothing.

It was not I who threw him over the cliff. We were walking one day and talking, and I noticed how he was ageing, though proud and angry like a king bull. The thought of bulls recalled my mind to Crete, and Crete to Minos; to a square throne, tight-waisted women, pinched Phædra, ropes, a grinning black Aphrodite-at-home, the north wind that comes ruffling our sea, loud voices, men with gold hair.

Then, as I was thinking, his foot slipped, and he was over the edge; and if I trod on his hand as it clung, well I was king again, like a tree that reclothes itself, year out, year in.

Only, to quiet all tumult in the city, I established his young children by Phædra at Scyros, and have given him the mound, the games, the libations, and cut tresses for a hero, even the Sacred Snake.

But it was I that put them there. Things may be equal between us. I leave it at that, as I have left other things.

Green

'**D**on't you think, Madonna Loring, that it would be better if I went down to see?'

'I'll think of it,' she said quickly, and he noticed a slight hauteur in her voice.

'We are sure, alas! that she takes too much to drink, and we know that my son does not. And you have heard what people say about her friends. Nick would never allow me to know the Taverners, so is it likely that he will have them to his house unless she insists? And if she does and he refuses, as he certainly should, she will fall out of her own set, and most of his friends will have nothing to do with her. The Derings have hinted to me that they might have to drop Nick. I hardly like to tell you, Ambrose, but they said –' A paraphrase followed for several sexual and social irregularities.

'Don't you think I might go?' Ambrose Alexander said this with loving earnestness, with whimsical adoration, leaning over a narrow space towards an old woman, upright by the fire in a dull-gold London room. Inside her tight silver wig and her mask of paint, she was yielding to treatment. In one hollow centimetre of her mind she knew she was, and that she would send Ambrose, because he would bring back an exciting story, a story that would justify malice and moral indignation: that could also be repudiated without strain. He owed her a good deal, she thought. He was a Jew. His function was to please. He did please. A slim, supple young man to run about was essential: to confide in: to reassure her.

For his part he was willing to oblige her. There were good pickings in that family, and benefits apart, she was giving him what he wanted – a chance to get his own back on her son and

71

his wife. For the six months before, for the six months since, their marriage, she had been ravenous for its discredit. The discredit it was for him to supply. But a full meal this time, and more than a meal, a provision, on which she would never satiate, of the wife's blood and sap. What she wanted would serve his turn; but when he thought about her, and he preferred not to think about her too much, he misunderstood her degrees of consciousness, the balance of her scruples, her ignorance, her appetite, and her fears.

'If you are to go down and see her, how can it be arranged? It mustn't look –'

'They had better not expect me. If I could have a car and it should break down, then I could simply be there, and they would put me up for the night.'

'That's a good idea. I'll pay for it. But, mind you, Ambrose, it must be a real breakdown. I won't have any lies.'

'Madonna Loring it shall go up in flames to make my word, since it is really your word, good.'

She looked away from him, a little sentimental smile disturbing the corners of the old thin mouth. If only in her life she had heard more men say things like that. He meant it. Ambrose was a good and noble man. Of course he would not have to burn the car. That would be too extravagant. Even for the most disgusting news of her daughter-in-law.

Splendid that Ambrose was going. Her son might be in agonies about his wife: her son might be wanting his home again. She would give Ambrose messages to make it easy for him to come home for help. She foresaw decent divorce, and when Ambrose was gone, walked up and down the long room between the azaleas and the inlaid chairs, rehearsing a long, hideous, and wholly satisfactory scene with his wife.

Until the nature of the interview from being a source of pleasure became a kind of pain, and she noticed that she was not sure how far she wanted to be able to trust Ambrose there. Later she rang him up.

'Of course I'll pay all your expenses, but don't be too extravagant. I've just thought we may need all our money later.'

She had said 'our money' out of romantic delicacy. Ambrose relished it differently. It had been share and share alike with

Nicholas, who usually forgot about his own share. Then, a year ago, Nicholas had found out that intermittent rebellion is exhausting, and had conducted an entire revolution instead. Six months later he was married. Now his landmarks were off both their maps. Only their débris remained – nothing but skeletons and broken boards where his places had been. A devastating escape, but Nick's mother had herself to thank. And hatred of his wife, which had been her refuge, was to become her revenge. Against Nancy Loring, Ambrose knew nothing – had not heard much – '*Le dossier accusateur de toute jolie femme.*' But to be kept by Mrs Loring; he must keep Mrs Loring; give Mrs Loring what she wanted, a daughter-in-law unkind, unchaste, and, so far as possible, unkissed. It seemed that he might have to rely on his imagination. After six months they were still living out of London, in that small, remote house, where no one that he knew ever went. Without a car, a telephone, or a horse. With cats and an old boat and books. That did not promise disillusion yet unless the girl was bored. What was there to find out? Could he return and report bliss? A spring wind filled the curtains of his room; coaldust from the unlit fire charged its delicate touch. With his eyes on the tree-tops breaking leaf he could only smell London. He did not particularly mind, but at night with the fire burning he could feel Mrs Loring behind his chair. Boards cracked before and after her tread, step of a bully with small feet and ankles swollen a little with age, and there was a sound of gobbling already, and appetite unglutted, and punishment for Nick shaping once she had got him back. Once they had got him back.

Need he go at all? Could he go in theory, or, if he went, in theory provoke Nancy to behaviour whose character could be decided on later, and Nick actually into appropriate disgust? There is nothing more difficult to deny than a casual event whose importance rests on its implications. It is said that you have been to Biarritz with friends of doubtful character.

You do not know the people.

You have not been to Biarritz at all.

Prove it, if you have not been conspicuously with other people anywhere else. The force of your denial will fly loose, attach itself, and strengthen the accusation. You will have been at St Jean de Luz, where you met, and were notorious with them there. It is this fact that lies at the base of all non-resistance to evil, that the resistance becomes a neutral agent, equally able to strengthen what it attacks.

Ambrose felt that he need not be too anxious. There is always something wrong. If it were not yet conscious he had only to give the unconscious a name. While it was equally possible that the girl was bored, loose, or a slut. If not, she was going to be. The elegantly set problem absorbed him, in whose solution he ignored himself, his emotion for Nick, his curiosity about Nancy, his fear of the mother – about whom he assumed himself to be particularly cynical and gay.

Two days later he ran out of petrol on a remote road a mile from their house.

Nancy Loring asked her husband: 'Who was it called the sea the "very green"?'

'The Egyptians, I think. The Red Sea and the Mediterranean. What about green wine?'

They were looking out at a green plain which lay as far as the horizon on their left, and their house stood on the shelf of a grass hill beside the plain, tilted in the sunlight to another green. High trees stood about the hill, and a short way outside, across a lawn, a copse crested its last bank. The plain had once been the sea, an estuary savage with tides, now narrowed to a river, tearing at its flow and ebb; where all winter, for every hundred yards, a heron watched its pitch. There was no dust: no sound but birds and air; no colour but green. There was every green.

In late April the top greens were of gold. Across the plain there was a march of elms, open hands with blood inside them, tipped with saffron fire. The copse was a stuff woven out of the same green.

They went out. On the small lawn were cats, black and white enamel in fur. One watched its lover; the lover watched a bird; the third, bow-stretched and upright, ripped the bark off a tree. Two kittens tumbled over like black and white flowers.

They followed one another through the copse. Each willow trunk was a separate man and woman. They came down the farther side to where, when it had been sea, the plain had worn a little bay under the hill. There was long wet grass where the tide-mark had been. They came to a dyke and an old house. There were willows along the glass water, very tall; along it and over it, one flung across and an elm tree drowned in it, its root out of the ground in a flat earth-cake. The house was a deserted farm. An orchard reached it, down a small valley between the rising of another hill. There was no path. They went up through the apple-trees, through a place wholly sheltered, where no wind came but only sun; where, when there was no sun, there was always light; so that in mid-winter, in the stripped world, the seasons did not exist there. They called it the Apple Land, remembering there something which they could not recall, that seemed to have the importance of a just-escaped dream. The orchard ended sharply in an overhanging quickset, and a sharp climb to the top of the hill. To follow the valley to its head there was a glen on the left, sickly with flies and thin shoots and a scummed choked stream up to a short fall, almost in the dark, which was not quite wholesome, whose pool was without stir or light. The way out of that was also sharp and steep but quite different – to a shut cottage on top and a garden with tansy in it, and herbs used in magic.

Through lambs running in the up-fields they came to their village, and bought a morning paper, cheese, apples, and cigarettes. They came back another way, by a highroad, by a lane, over the open grass along a ribbon their feet had printed, green upon green.

Ambrose Alexander reached the house as they had entered the copse. A shy country servant left him alone. He was pleased that they were out; he stood back by the door from where he could see the whole length of the room.

Across the table an open ordnance map hung like a cloth askew. There was a chessboard beside it, and men half tumbled out of a box, and a wide bowl of small mixed flowers. There was a stone bottle of ink and a dish with sticks of sealing-wax and stamps, pencils, and a seal. There was a dog's lead and a pair of leather gloves. A red handkerchief was knotted up full of needles and wool. When he handled it one ran into his palm. There was an

oil painting of Mount Soracte and steel prints of forgotten gentlemen; and on the black chimney-shelf a fishing-rod crossed with
a gun. There were books of poems, and on murder, the Roman
occupation of Britain, Chinese art.

*Mr Hunca Munca, the mouse, climbed to the top of the kitchen
chimney and looked out. There was no soot.* Up to the age of five
every child laughs at this version of that joke; but to Ambrose it
was as if the room was calling him, very plainly and in another
language, an outsider. It was not what he had come to hear. He
stared out of the window and up the hill. There was no one. Then
he went upstairs. Under his feet the old boards had no friendly
squeak. Like old servants who might talk.

Their bedroom had a rose-brick fireplace and a line of Persian
prints. Under the mirror, piled in a shell, were strings of glass
flowers and fruit. Everything was in order, polished and very still,
and the bathroom full of things to wash with. He went back to
the bedroom, supposed that in one of the shut drawers there was
a shameful secret among soiled linen, persuaded himself, opened
it, and in it there were folded silks, bedroom books: two more
murders, a County History, *Per Amica Silentia Lunæ*, Sterne. A
cat looked in at the door and yawned before it went away. Under
a scent-flask was a receipted bill. He looked out of the window
at the very green.

There they had been all winter long. They did not seem to
want to go away. Told nothing, saw no one who would tell anything, asked for nothing. He was discouraged. Propriety, simplicity, the routine of country-house life. The house went on talking
out loud; not without passion but with directness that annihilated.
Down any passage there might be met a wall of fire. He looked
at the bed over whose foot-rail hung a bright shawl and a fur.

The Persian pictures were perfectly proper. In the dining-room
cupboard there had been two bottles of beer. He went downstairs,
heard no approach on the soundless turf, so that they were on
him in an instant, as instantly recoiled, and a moment later were
overwhelmed in his cordiality and excuse.

Disentangling themselves from him, they exchanged a word
together, out of the house. 'What has he come for? Car broken
down? Whose car? Who's given him a car?'

Nicholas Loring was annoyed; his wife uneasy. There was

nothing to do but feed him, and not go after the swan's nest that day. Swans stay put, but are more interesting than a townsman ill at ease, vocal and supple and full of admiration that did not try to be more than a display. Voluble and mobile, Ambrose had a trick of statement, one to each sentence, followed by a denial, a reversal of it in the next. So that which seemed, sentence by sentence, to be a vivid reaction to life, cancelled out to nothing. To no belief at all. Nicholas, folded-up in country quiet, was now without illusion and irritated by what had once stimulated him. Ambrose had no belief at all. And Nancy saw that everything Ambrose said would mean nothing, and felt giddy in her mind until she felt sick. They were his hosts and they must stomach him, feed him, and endure him to an hour that had not fixed. They were saved from spiritless irritation, and she from fear, by curiosity and the involuntary hosts' calculation of the time when they would be able to lose him. Ambrose understood this, and that he must stay the night, and that at present no mere breakdown of his car would get him the invitation. He saw himself after lunch led by Nick, grim, courteous, and embarrassed, to restart it at the top of the hill.

They came to the end of lunch. Nicholas was listening to Ambrose, to what he had once heard, year in year out, and now had not heard for a year. And after a year there was no more pleasure in it or surprise at the changes. It was as if he knew it by heart, for the first time at last.

Ambrose was trying hard with a parade of emotion, trying to praise marriage, their withdrawal, the serene country; displaying himself as the neurotic townsman, the alien, whose pride it was to humble himself, to look into paradise through bars. A peep he owed to them: 'Is that safe, Nancy?' turning to her from Nicholas.

'I think so,' she answered civilly, not at all sure. 'He is trying not to cancel out,' she thought. 'Why? He can't do it for long. Why is he here? He does not like me. Would like me to be vile so as to hurt Nick. Nick he loves and hates. Then that he had once loved Nick and then hated him, probably for his marriage and now did neither, or in different proportions. What was he there for?'

He said: 'Suppose me at my role again – the old serpent. You used, Nick, to call me that, and any variation that struck you from "you dirty devil" to "Lucifer".'

'Lord of lies,' she murmured.

He heard her. She was ashamed. He looked steadily at her and smiled. 'You're right, my dear. I'm just as much that variation of the fiend. Only neither you nor Nick need the serpent in me any more. Serpents' – he added – 'are not sentimental. That was useful once to Nick. While who has ever heard of a mother-snake?' They took that in.

'There was a time when Nick needed an old, contradictory bloke like me to leave all doors open and let a spot of reality in. His mother' (the pause which left her unqualified perfected suggestion) 'she would have shut the lot, and everything open is the only answer to everything shut. But now –' He went on to explain that Nicholas, now he had welcomed the reality Ambrose had provided, had made his own freedom and been given love. It was true. But Nicholas must be repersuaded that he owed it to him. Doors that have been opened can be shut. One implies the other. They could begin on him again, he and Mrs Loring, and Nick would be well retrapped. The doors would be shut and the wife outside. Only it would take longer than he thought, and Mrs Loring would not see the delicacy of it. He must find out how to persuade her that the cup of deferred blood is richer.

Rapt in these thoughts he started smiling at them. Nick was moved, but remembered that once he would only have been moved. Ambrose had opened doors once, or he had thought so. Until he had noticed that he had slammed them to and fro, chasing him between draughts. Until he had stuck open a certain number that he needed for himself. (Who wants to live with every door open?) His exits and entrances were now his own, and by one of them Nancy had come in: helped to fix open a few more, and, by one of these, first Ambrose, then his mother, had gone out. That was what had happened in terms of doors. He softened, feeling that he could afford to. Old Ambrose had come down for some sort of thanks. Or perhaps for a share. Share of the rich strength which made things easy with Nancy: easy to give and take: easy to go in and out: to live: like music, all the musics. Ambrose was by himself as he'd always been. Nancy was thinking the same thing, that here was a man alone all his life and always would be alone; and thought of him on a toadstool and with people round him on toadstools, and that he spent his time picking their stalks from underneath them and his own stalk.

Then the strength mounting in her also, she wondered if Ambrose had been necessary to Nicholas, to that woman's only son. Was it possible that they had shaken Ambrose off his fence? Was this visit, after all, a no mean congratulation and praise; one of the mysterious triumphs of love? She forgot his subtle opposition to their marriage. Was this old Mrs Loring's last defeat? She judged it most improbable and forgot her judgment. Only remembered that it would be good if it were true. If it were true, they might some day be able to forgive. She looked at Ambrose, very simply. It seemed a far cry to 'mother's gigolo'. He observed her, went to the piano, and played the letter-song from *Figaro*. Whistling softly. *And the sounds of beauty flowed and trembled until they seemed to triumph... over the hard hearts of men.*

She brought him over his coffee. There was not a cruel animal behind Nick, only a vexed old woman, who had been lovely, who would never feed on her son again, or with septic finger-nails scratch at the bloom of her own youth. She had been ungenerous about Ambrose. How hateful is the wife who does injustice to her husband's people, to her husband's friends.

She lit his cigarette, and stood by Nicholas' shoulder, wholly herself and part of him and part of the very green. Part of Ambrose? Yes, for this moment, if this were true.

They took him out, a tramp across green, from green to green, entertained him with birds' nests set deep in thorned twigs and split light. There had been tea and toast and chess, an evening to get through and a night. He stood between them at evening at the door of the house. Now in the sky there was a bar of the green that has no name. He was standing on grass darkening beside dark green. She had said, '*It is all Hermes, all Aphrodite.*'

He had been bored and concealed it, with the night before him, becoming unsure of himself. Dinner, chess, music, country-talk. A drink? They had filled up his car and put her away in the village and refused to let him go.

They gave him a drink and a rabbit cooked in onions. He had gained nothing but the fooling of them, and if they did not know it, they were slightly bored. The worst thing that can happen to a liar is to be believed. If he did not notice that, he suffered, as Nick indicated in intimate outline, his serene and final detachment from his mother. Confident, they told him their plans, about excavations and gardening, and Nick's new book, which was not about himself or even about people. He had to listen, and by that time it was night, grey, windless, with a squeak in it. The great chimney flared. Standing inside it one could follow the sparks up its square tower to a square patch of sky. Innocent as wine, as dew. He sneered. Outside was it innocent? Innocent for them and strong. His room was away from theirs. On that side of the house the night could do what it liked with him. The night would have him to itself. Nick and Nancy would have themselves to themselves. He would have nothing to himself but himself and night. Oh! there was someone who might come in and sit beside his bed. Madame Nick might come in and talk, smile, and suck in her thin, red lips. Keep him awake because she was hungry. She would not mind dark green night.

He would have nothing but lies to feed her on: have to invent her a meal because her sort of food wasn't in the house. He was getting childish. With their stupid innocence they were doing him down. What did Nancy want? To give him another drink: be sure that he was comfortable: a game of chess before bed. 'Glorious game,' he must say, but it took longer to play than he reckoned. A shy woman, what she did was better than her promise. Later she said: 'It is good for your complexes, Ambrose, to win things and be praised.' For that he should have let her win. God! But he could not bear to evade the game. And it put off bed, and whatever it was that tapped outside on the windows its peculiar code.

But when he went up, the soft air surging in put him instantly to sleep.

They woke next morning with a distaste for him in the house. He was to go after lunch, and the morning seemed an hour-series that could not be lived through. There was no reason for it, only that they did not care now if his visit marked a triumph. They wanted him out of the way. There were interesting things to do and he would not do them. Nancy decided that she would disappear, on the excuse of leaving Nicholas alone with his friend, and came downstairs first to see that Ambrose had his breakfast in bed. There was a letter for her from Nick's mother. That hardly ever happened. She went outside to read it, barefoot on the cat-printed dew: split it open and read:

My Dear Child,

I wish this to be entirely between ourselves, but I have an idea that Nicholas' old friend Ambrose intends to come down and see you. Please be very nice to him. You know how he is – he was so fond of my son and has suffered the break since his marriage. Of course it couldn't be helped, and I am so afraid of emotional friendships between young men, but I am sure you have nothing to fear now. Don't tell Nicholas anything about this – and also what I meant to say is – don't be upset or offended if he should try and flirt with you. It means absolutely nothing. He has a very fine nature really, and is not at all interested in women. I just want there to be no misunderstanding, not that Nicholas is likely to think anything as long as you are careful, only I do not wish you for your part to be led away. I explain this badly, but I am sure you will understand. I hope you are both as well as possible.

Your loving Mother,

Angela Loring

The crisp dew melted between her toes, and their colour changed from pink to red. One hand held on to her curled, cropped hair. There was a moment when nothing happened at all, neither image nor concept nor sense impression. She came-to, first to the small bustling wind, then to a bird. Then to a draught of other life-like voices, shrieking from London, recorded on a square of thick white paper. It was mad; it was comic; it was dangerous. She ate a light breakfast in silence. Anyhow it was tiresome.

She said: 'You will want the morning with Ambrose. I'm off.' But Nicholas had his plans also.

'Look here,' he said. 'I forgot that I said that I'd see that man about –'

'Take him with you.'

'It's a trudge. I got mud to my knees last –'

'Am I to keep Ambrose?'

'I mean, if you could be that sort of spirit – I'll be back before lunch.'

'Very well. Do you mind what happens to him?'

'I'm leaving him with you –' He grinned, and there began to be less of him, a hand or an ear or a foot left, and the rest out of sight, and then the whole of him out of reach.

After she had been alone for ten minutes she began to feel holy, and inside herself an immense preoccupation with power. She went upstairs, put on a gayer sweater, and delicately painted her face. So Ambrose had come down to see if there was anything to be done about Nick. Through her. If she had been easy, to have her; easy or discontented or jealous of Nick. Very likely Mrs Loring, Mère Angélique, had sent him herself and repented, and so written. She had thought such a thing possible? Wanted such a thing? Wanted her son's wife a slut and had not wanted it. Wanted Ambrose back? In her mind there was the old woman's name written-up and scored through. Then she went out and called lightly up at his window from the cool lawn.

'Come down, Ambrose, it's a perfect day.'

With sweet animation and pretty phrases she made Nick's excuses, and took him the plain way up the hill to the village for a drink.

He had better go, he thought, there was nothing doing here. He was separated after the night's deep sleep, cut off already from what had been yesterday's preoccupations, and those of weeks and years and even of a life past. Indifferent for the moment to their reassertion, like a man drugged, but not as though it was well with him there. So that the only thing was to get away. Go before lunch and cut its pointless coda. God! was Nancy, the woman beside him, talking, running a primrose through his coat, trying to flirt with him at last? The gentle admiration of last night turned pert with a grin behind it. She went on like that all the way to the village inn. He had a drink. He needed it. He was imagining things. She was a gay baggage after all, and he'd interested her. She wanted to know about himself, did she? She'd got rid of Nick. What was she saying?

'It's good of you to tolerate me, Ambrose. After you and Nick. What a marvellous friendship we might have. But oh, my dear –!'

'What do you do me the honour of thinking about me, wife of Nicholas?' There was another drink before him. Put it down. It was quick work following this up.

'This visit has cleared up so much, made almost anything possible. And now we are friends, I feel I must say anything to you that I think.'

'Go on.'

'Anything? You mean it? Then Ambrose, I shall begin about yourself; and first of all I'm going to tell you something you're to do and that you are not to do.'

'I'll obey you.' Her voice had light music in it.

Now she leaned across the inn table, *dulce ridentem*, a shadow in her smile, making him aware of her awareness of him.

'You are a great man, Ambrose, but oh, *mon ami*, love Nicholas, love me, but don't, don't –'

'What am I not to do, lady of the place?'

'You should not, you must not. Ambrose, you are not to let people call you – you are not to be so mixed up – with old women who exploit you. I'm a woman, and I'm not an old woman, but do you know what some old women are like? They adore your looks and your sweet manners, and,' she added rudely, 'how? They want you physically, of course, but not simply physically; and they've their own way of getting that. And when they've got what they want, or not got what they want, then they make comparisons.'

What was this? She was serious, she was smiling. There was a smile set against him and eyes lit with cold fun.

'Whatever dowager takes such an interest in me?'

'Oh, my dear, with so many about, and you so liked and hard-up. Why, this morning I had a letter from Nick's mother, for you to be returned intact. A perfectly wolfish howl. How did she know you were here?' The smiles were working easily on her lips, but her eyes were steady. Steady as two carved stones on rock.

'I think you should be kind to her; kind as you are to Nick; kind as you are to me.'

She was making a sing-song of it, her head drawn up, her throat strained a little under the high collar of bright wool. Then relaxing: 'Forgive this candour,' she said; 'I know how they can be useful, these women. Only if you can't do without them, you must learn how to keep them in order. Nick was a little annoyed that his mother should write such a letter. Keep her in hand. You remember about Peter Carmin and how his friends got him out of the country –'

If she had been alone down there with him at the house she would not have been safe, in spite of the green.

'May I see the letter?' (He must say that.)

'Nick has it.' That was what she must say. She could say what she liked. She was in her own land. It was then that she heard his surrender.

'Tell Nick I will write to him. I think I had better go up now since the car is here.'

Its noise drowned her light farewells and excuses.

She dropped back softly between the hills, by the first way, through the Apple-Land. Round the green bay, through the copse, until outside the house she was looking at the plain and the trees' open hands. Her husband came suddenly round a corner of the house and saw that she was alone.

'Gone,' she said; 'and before I come in take this letter into the house and read it.'

With and Without Buttons

It is not only true, it is comforting, to say the incredulity is often no more than superstition turned inside out. But there can be a faith of disbelief as inaccurate as its excess, and in some ways more trying, for the right answers to it have not yet been thought up. It was only because Trenchard said at lunch that the mass was a dramatized wish-fulfilment that what came after ever happened. At least I wish we did not think so. It was trying to get out anyhow, but if he had not irritated us and made us want to show off, we would not have made ourselves serviceable to it. And it was we who came off lightly. To him it has been something that he has not been able to shake off. When it happened he behaved so well about it, but that didn't save him. Now he cannot think what he used to think, and he does not know what else there is that he might think.

I am seeing him now, more vividly than I like. He was our next-door neighbour in a remote village in Kent. A nest of wasps had divided their attention between us, and we had met after sunset to return their calls with cyanide and squibs.

He was a sanguine man, positive, hearty, actually emotional. He had known and done a great many things, but when he came to give his account of them, all he had to say was a set of pseudo-rationalizations, calling the bluff, in inaccurate language, of God, the arts, the imagination, the emotions. That is not even chic science for laymen today. He might have thought that was as much as he liked, but there was no reason, we said, to try and prove it to us all one hot, sweet, blue-drawn summer, in a Kentish orchard; to sweat for our conversion; to shame us into agreement. Until the evening I told him to stop boring us with his wish-fulfilments, for they weren't ours, and saw his healthy skin start to sweat and a stare come into his eyes. That ought to have warned me, as it did my sister, of whom I am sometimes afraid. It did warn us, but it wound us up also. We went home through the orchard in the starlight and sat downstairs in the midsummer night between lit candles, inviting in all that composed it, night hunting cries and scents of things that grow and ripen, cooled in the star-flow. A world visible, but not in terms of colour. With every door and every window open, the old house was no more than a frame, a set of screens to display night, midsummer, perfume, the threaded stillness, the stars strung together, their spears glancing, penetrating an earth breathing silently, a female power asleep.

'All he hears is nature snoring,' said my sister. 'Let's give him a nightmare.' It was a good idea.

'How?' I said.

'We'll find out tomorrow. I can feel one about.' I got up to close the doors before we mounted with our candles. Through walls and glass, through open doors or shut, a tide poured in, not of air or any light or dark or scent or sound or heat or coolness. Tide. Without distinction from north or south or without or within; without flow or ebb, a Becoming; without stir or departure or stay: without radiance or pace. Star-tide. Has not Science had wind of rays poured in from interstellar space?

There is no kind of ill-doing more fascinating than one which has a moral object, a result in view which will justify the means without taking the fun out of them. All that is implied when one says that one will give someone something to cry about. It was that line which we took at breakfast.

'We'll try his simple faith,' we said. 'We'll scare him stiff and see how he stands the strain. We'll haunt him.' And asked each other if either of us knew of a practising vampire in the neighbourhood or a were-cow.

It was several days before we hit on a suitable technique, examining and rejecting every known variety of apparition, realizing that apparatus must be reduced to a minimum, and that when nothing will bear scrutiny, there must be very little given to scrutinize. In fact, what we meant to do was to suggest him into an experience – the worse the better – wholly incompatible with the incredulities of his faith. That it would be easy to do, we guessed; that it would be dangerous to him – that appeared at the moment as part of the fun. Not because we did not like him, but because we wanted to have power over him, the power women sometimes want to have over men, the pure, not erotic power, whose point is that it shall have nothing to do with sex. We could have made him make love, to either or both of us, any day of the week.

This is what we planned, understanding that, like a work of art, once it had started, its development could be left to look after itself.

'Suppose,' said my sister, 'that we have heard a ridiculous superstition in the village that there is Something Wrong with the house. We will tell him that, and when he has gone through his reaction exercises – it may take a day or so and will depend on our hints, and if we make the right ones, the battle's won – he will ask us what the story is.'

'What is it to be?' I said, who can rarely attain to my sister's breadth of mind.

'That does not matter. Because before we begin we'll *do* something. Anything. A last year's leaf for a start, so long as it can go into a series – on his blotter or his pillow. We're always in and out. We'll put them there and get asked round for the evening and start when we see one, and that's where our village story begins. All that he has to get out of us is that there *is* a story, and that wet leaves or whatever it is we choose are found about. Signatures, you know. If he doesn't rise the first night, he'll find that leaf when he goes to bed. It depends on how well we do it –'

I recognized a master's direction, but it all seemed to depend on our choice of stimulants. Last year's leaves, delicate damp articulations; coloured pebbles, dead flies, scraps of torn paper with half a word decipherable.... A mixture of these or a selection?

'Keep it tangible,' my sister said – 'that's the way. Our only difficulty is the planting of them.'

'Which,' I asked, 'are suitable to what?' It seemed to be necessary in laying our train to determine the kind of unpleasantness for which they were ominous. But I could not get my sister to attend.

'It's not that way round,' she said at length – 'dead bees, feathers, drops of candle-grease? Old kid gloves? With and Without Buttons. That will do.'

I felt a trifle queer. 'Well,' I said, 'they're the sort of things a man never has in his house, so that's sound so far. But women do. Not the sort of things we wear, but he'd not know that. And how do we get hold of them?'

'There's a shoe-box in the loft full of them, by the door into his place when these houses were one.' (Our cottages were very old, side by side, with a common wall, our orchards divided by a hedge.) We had rented ours from a friend who had recently bought it as it stood from a local family which had died out, and of which very little seemed known. My sister said:

'Shiny black kid and brown, with little white glass buttons and cross stitching and braid. All one size, and I suppose for one pair of hands. Some have all the buttons and some have none and some have some –' I listened to this rune until I was not sure how many times my sister had said it.

'With and without buttons,' I repeated, and could not remember how often I had said that.

After that we said nothing more about it, and it was three days later that he asked us to supper, and we walked round through the gap in the hedge in the pure daylight, and sat in his little verandah, whose wooden pillars spread as they met the roof in fans of plaited green laths. Prim fantasy, with its french windows behind it, knocked out of walls of flint rubble three feet thick. Roses trailed up it. A tidy little home, with something behind it of monstrous old age one did as well to forget.

'By the way,' he said. (As I have said before, his name was Trenchard, and he had come back to his own part of England to rest, after a long time spent in looking after something in East Africa.) 'By the way, have either of you two lost a glove?'

'So she's got busy already and didn't tell me, the spoil sport,' I thought.

'No,' we said, 'but one always does. What sort of a glove?'

'A funny little thing of brown kid with no buttons. I didn't think it could be yours. I found it on the top of the loft stairs. Outside the door. Here it is.' He went inside and came out on to the verandah where we were having supper, a moment later, puzzled.

'Here it is,' he said. 'I put it in the bureau, and the odd thing is that when I went to look for it I found another. Not its pair either. This one's black.'

Two little lady-like shiny kid gloves, the kind worn by one's aunts when one was a child. I had not yet seen our collection. The black had three of its buttons missing. We told him that they were not the kind that women wore now.

'My landlady bought the place furnished,' he said. 'Must have come out of the things the old owners left behind when they died.' My sister gave a slight start, a slight frown and bit her lip. I shook my head at her.

'What's up?' he asked, simply.

'Nothing,' we said.

'I'm not going to be laughed at by you,' said my sister.

'I'm not laughing,' he said, his goodwill beaming at us, prepared even to be tolerant.

'Oh, but you'd have the right to –'

After that, he wanted to know at once.

'It's playing into your hands,' she said, 'but don't you know that your half of the house is the Village Haunt? And that it's all about gloves? With and without buttons?'

It was ridiculously easy. He was amiable rather than irritated at her story, while I was still hurt that she had not first rehearsed it with me. She began to tell him a story about old Miss Blacken, who had lived here with her brother, a musty old maid in horrible clothes, but nice about her hands; and how there was something – no, not a ghost – but something which happened that was always preceded by gloves being found about. This we told him and he behaved very prettily about it, sparing us a lecture.

'But it's not quite fair,' he said. 'I mustn't be selfish. She must leave some at your place. Remember, in her day, it was all one house.'

Then we talked about other things, but when we had gone home I found my sister a little pensive. I began on my grievance.

'Why didn't you tell me you had begun? Why didn't you coach me?' Then she said:

'To tell you the truth, I hadn't meant to begin. What I said I made up on the spot. All I'd done was that just before we left I ran up to the loft and snatched a glove from the box and left it on his bureau. That's the second one he found.'

'Then what about the one he found outside the loft door?'

'It's that that's odd. That's why he never thought it was us. I haven't had a chance to get to that part of his house. I didn't put it there.'

Well, now that the affair was launched, we felt it had better go on. Though I am not sure if we were quite so keen about it. It was as though – and we had known this to be possible before – it had already started itself. One sometimes feels this has happened. Anyhow, it was two days later before I thought it was my turn to lay a glove on his premises, and went up to our loft and took one out of the box. There was nothing in it but gloves. I took a white one, a little cracked, with only two buttons, and having made sure he was out, slipped through the hedge and dropped it at the foot of the stair. He startled me considerably by returning at that instant. I said I had come for a book. He saw the thing.

'Hullo,' he said, 'there's another. It's beginning. That makes four.'

'Four?' I said. 'There were only two the other night.'

'I found one in my bedroom. A grey. Are we never going to get a pair?'

Then it occurred to me that he'd seen through us all along, and was getting in ahead with gloves. I took my book and returned to my sister.

'That won't do,' she said, 'he's sharp, but we didn't begin it. He found his first.'

I said: 'I'm beginning to wonder if it mightn't be a good thing to find out in the village if anything is known about Miss Blacken and her brother.'

'You go,' said my sister, still pensive.

I went to the pub when it opened and drew blank. I heard about diseases of bees and chickens and the neighbours. The Post Office was no good. I was returning by a detour, along a remote lane, when a voice said:

'You *were* asking about Miss Blacken along at Stone Cottages?'

It was only a keeper who had been in the pub, come up suddenly through a gate, out of a dark fir planting. '– Seeing as you have the uses of her furniture,' said he. We passed into step. I learned that after fifty years' odd residence in the place there was nothing that you might have to tell about her and waited.

'– Now her brother, he was not what you might call ordinary.' Again that stopped at that.

'– Regular old maid she was. If maid she'd ever been. Not that you could be saying regular old man for him, for he wasn't either, if you take my meaning, Miss.'

I did. Finally I learned – and I am not quite sure how I learned – it was certainly not all by direct statement – that Miss Blacken had been a little grey creature, who had never seemed naturally to be living or dying; whose clothes were little bits and pieces, as you might say. Anyhow, she'd dropped something – an excuse me, Miss, petticoat, his wife had said – on the green, and run away without stopping to pick it up, opening and shutting her mouth. It was then it had begun. If you could call *that* beginning. I was asking to know what that was? In a manner of speaking he couldn't rightly say. It was the women took it to heart. What became of the petticoat? That was the meaning of it. 'Twasn't rightly speaking a petticoat at all. There weren't no wind, and when they came to pick it up, it upped and sailed as if there were a gale of wind behind it, right out of sight along the sky. And one day it had come back; hung down from the top of an elm and waved at them, and the women had it there were holes in it, like a face. And no wonder, seeing it had passed half a winter blowing about in the tops of the trees. Did it ever come down to earth? Not it they said. Nor old Miss Blacken start to look for it, except that it was then that people remembered her about at nights.

A little pensive now myself, I asked about gloves and was told and no more than that 'they say that she's left her gloves about'.

I returned to my sister and we spent the evening doing a reconstruction of Miss Blacken out of Victorian oddments. It was most amusing and not in the least convincing.

'Tomorrow, shall we feed him a glove?' I said. It was then that it came across our minds, like a full statement to that effect, that it was no longer necessary. The gloves would feed themselves.

'I know what it is we've done,' said my sister, 'we've wound it up.'

'Wound up what?' I answered. 'Ghost of a village eccentric, who was careful about her hands?'

'Oh no,' said my sister. 'I don't know. Oh no.'

After another three days, I said:

'Nothing more has happened over there. I mean he's found no more gloves. Hadn't we better help things along a bit?'

'There was one yesterday in my room, unbuttoned,' she said. 'I didn't drop it.'

I was seriously annoyed. This seemed to be going too far. And in what direction? What does one do when this sort of thing happens? I was looking as one does when one has heard one's best friend talking about oneself, when the shadow of a heavy man fell across our floor. It was Trenchard. My sister looked up and said quickly:

'We've found one now.'

'Have you?' he said. 'So have I.' He hesitated. There was something very direct and somehow comforting in the way he was taking it, piece by piece as it happened, not as what he would think it ought to mean. It was then that we began to be ashamed of ourselves. He went on:

'You know my cat. She's her kittens hidden somewhere in the loft and I wanted to have a look at them. I went up softly not to scare her. You know it's dark on that top stair. I got there, and then I heard – well – a little thing falling off a step. Thought it was a kitten trying to explore. Peered and felt and picked up a glove.'

He pulled it out of his pocket and held it up by a finger with slight distaste. A brown one this time.

'One button,' he said. 'The kittens aren't big enough to have been playing with it and the cat wasn't about. There's no draught. Funny, isn't it? Reminded me of one of those humpty-dumpty toys we had, a little silk man with arms and legs and a painted face, and a loose marble inside him to make him turn over and fall about.'

My sister said:

'We've found a box of loose gloves in our attic close to your bricked-up door.'

His answer was that it was bricked up all right, and had we thought to count them in case either of our maids was up to some village trick. We hadn't, but I noticed that he mistrusted our maids as little as we did. Also that his behaviour was so reasonable because he had not yet thought that there was any cause for suspicion.

'Let's do it now,' he said. 'Put them all back, yours and mine. Count them and lock your door.'

He went back and fetched his five, and together we went upstairs. They sat on a basket trunk while I emptied the box.

'Twenty-seven. Eleven pairs in all and one missing.' I shovelled them back into the cardboard box, yellow with time and dust. I looked up at his broad straight nose and my sister's little one that turns up. Both were sniffing.

'There's a smell here,' they said. There was. Not the dust-camphor-mouse-and-apple smell proper to lofts.

'I know what it is,' Trenchard said, 'smelt it in Africa in a damp place. Bad skins.'

The loft went suddenly darker. We looked up. There was no window, but someone had cut the thatch and let in a skylight. Something was covering it, had suddenly blown across it, though outside there was no wind. I took the iron handle with holes in it to stick through the pin in the frame, and threw it up. The piece of stuff slid backwards into the thatch. I put my arm out, caught hold of it and pulled it in. A piece of calico with a stiff waxy surface, once used for linings, again some time ago. It seemed to have no shape, but there were holes in it. Holes not tears.

'Nasty slummy rag,' I said. 'I suppose it was lying about in the thatch.'

Our thatch was old and full of flowers. This thing went with dustbins and tin cans. One piece was clotted together. A large spider ran out of it. I dropped it on the floor beside the box and the gloves. I was surprised to see Trenchard look at it with disgust.

'Never could stand seeing things go bad,' he said. We left the attic, locking the door and went downstairs. We gave him the key. It seemed the decent thing to do.

Over a late and thoughtful tea, we talked of other things. We did not think it necessary to tell him what the keeper had said.

The evening was exquisite and the next day and the next night. Days refreshed with night-showers to draw out scent, and steady sun to ripen; a pattern on the world like the dry dew on a moth's wing, or the skin on a grape or a rose. And nothing more happened. The next evening Trenchard was to give a little party for his birthday, for some friends who would motor over; and my sister and I were to see that all was in order for it, flowers and fruit and wine and all the good cold things to eat. We had the delicate pleasant things to do; to slice the cucumbers and drench sprays of borage and balm-in-Gilead for the iced drinks. The almonds did not come, so we salted some ourselves, blanching them in the garden, getting hot in the kitchen over pans of burnt salt.

At about six o'clock we went back to dress. Trying, as was appropriate, to look like Paris, in compliment to Trenchard, but principally to the garden and to the weather and to the earth. There was a bump overhead from the attic.

'What's that?' said my sister, painting her face.

'I left the skylight open,' I said. 'It must have slipped. Let's leave it. Am I in a state of dress or undress to go up there?'

She was ready before I was, and said that she was going across to Trenchard's to have one more look to see if all was in order there. Half of our day's work had been to keep him out of the way. We had just sent him up to the village after more strawberries and hoped that he would be back in time – and there was still plenty of time – for him to dress. As she went, I heard his step at his front door, and a few moments later, my dressing finished, I went downstairs and out across the orchard to join them. He had gone upstairs to change, but just as I reached the verandah, I heard a short cry which must have come from him. I ran in with my sister, who was also outside, building a last pyramid of strawberries on a dish shaped like a green leaf. He came out of the dining room.

'Who's done this?' he said.

The supper-table was set with food to be fetched and eaten when people pleased. There were little bowls of cut-glass set with sweets and almonds. One of these had been sprinkled with buttons, little white buttons that had been torn off, still ragged with red-brown threads.

'I filled it,' said my sister in a small weak voice, 'with those sugar rose leaves, and a real one on top.'

'Your servant –' I began, when he cried out again:

'What's that glove doing up the back of your dress?'

It was a little silver coat I had on to begin with. I pulled it off, and there fell off the collar, but with a tiny thud, another glove, a black one. It had no buttons on it and was open like a hand. Trenchard picked it up, and I thought I saw it collapse a little.

'No time to count them tonight,' he said, and looked round. It was too hot for a fire, but they were laid in all the rooms. He put the glove down and struck a match. The huge chimney used to roar with its draught, but the fire would not catch. He went out to the lavatory with the glove and the dish.

'Go up and dress,' we said when he came back; but instead he sniffed.

'It's what we smelt the other day,' he said. 'Up in the loft. Dead skin.'

Outside the air was hot and sweet and laced with coolness, but we noticed that here indoors it was cold, stale cold.

'Go and dress,' we said again, with the female instinct to keep the minutiæ of things steady and in sequence.

'They won't be here till eight: there's plenty of time,' he said, feeling not fear or even much curiosity, but that it was not the proper thing to leave us alone with the inexplicable unpleasant.

'Your servant,' I began again.

'My servant's all right,' he said. 'Go out and wait in the verandah. I'll be down quickly.'

So he went up. We took a chair and sat each side of the open glass doors where we could see into the house. We remembered that his maid as well as ours had gone back to her cottage to get ready for company. So there was no one in either house.

'He's taking it well,' we said, and 'What is it?' And what we meant was: 'What have we stirred up?' And (for my sister and I cannot lie to one another) 'You did not do that with the buttons in the dish?' 'Dear God, I did not.'

'A dirty old woman,' said my sister, 'nice about her hands.'

I said: 'Dirty things done in a delicate way. There was that piece of stuff.'

The house and the little orchard were backed with tall trees.

There was a hint of evening, and high branches black against strong gold. Was there something hanging high up, very high, that looked like a square of stuff that had holes in it?

Upstairs, Trenchard must have gone to the bathroom first. Then we heard him, moving about in his bedroom, just above the verandah roof. Then we heard him shout again, a cry he tried to stop. We ran out across the grass and called up at his window. He answered: 'No, don't come up.' Of course we ran up, in and through the sitting-room and up the stairs. The dining-room was still open, and with a corner of my eye I saw a candle, guttering hideously in the windless room.

'Let us in,' we said at his door.

'Of all the filthy nonsense –' he was repeating '– Look at my shirt.'

On the top of the chest of drawers out of which he had taken it, his shirt was lying; and on its stiff white linen was what looked like a patch of grey jelly. Only it had spread out from a clot into five ribbons, like a hand or the fingers of a glove.

'Fine sort of beastliness,' he said, 'that won't let you dress for dinner.' I heard myself saying:

'Are all your shirts like that?'

'No,' he said grimly, 'and if you don't mind waiting here till I've finished, we'll go downstairs and see what this is about.'

He took another shirt and finished his dressing, wincing as he touched things; while we felt as if there were slugs about, the things of which we are most afraid; and that we must keep our long dresses tight about us.

We went down together into the dining-room, and there my sister screamed. On the top of the centre strawberry pyramid, hanging over the berries like a cluster of slugs, was a glove, yellow-orange kid-skin, still and fat. A colour we had not seen in the box. The wrist and the fingers open and swollen. No buttons.

'What witches' trick is this?' he cried, and stared at us, for we were women. And like a wave moving towards us, rearing its head, came the knowledge that we were responsible for this; that our greed and vanity in devising this had evoked this: that we would now have to show courage, courage and intelligence to put an end to this, to lay this. And we had no idea how.

'The fire must burn,' I said. 'A great fire.' He turned towards the outhouse.

'What's that lovely scent you wear?' he said to my sister. – 'I want to smell it. Get that.'

She ran away, and I stood still, aware of my shoulder-blades and the back of my neck, and all of my body that I couldn't *see*. Doors would not open easily. I heard him swearing and stumbling, the clang of a bucket tripped over and kicked away in the yard. My sister ran in, a scent-spray in her hand, crying:

'It's not scent any more. I tried it. It smells like the attic –'

She was squeezing the bulb and spraying us all violently; and I could not smell the dead smell of the loft, but the sweetness, like a lady-like animal, of old kid gloves.

Outside, the delicious evening was pouring in, to meet the original smell of the house; smell of flowers and tobacco, of polished furniture and wood-smoke and good things to eat. Trenchard had brought in a gallon jar of paraffin. He tipped and splashed it over the sitting-room fire.

'Get all the gloves,' he said, looking at our helpless skirts: 'I'll go across. I've got the loft key.'

We peered again into the dining-room, that the kitchen opened out of. The candle guttered in fat dripping folds; a spider ran across a plate. My sister said:

'It's got only five fingers. Like a glove.'

We waited. 'Let's have the fire ready,' we said, and I staggered with the can at arm's length to the sitting-room fire and drenched the piled wood. The ugly vulgar smell was sweet with reassurance. My sister threw in a match. A roar drowned the crackle of catching sticks.

'Now for it,' we said, and tore open the bureau drawer for the gloves. I ran up for Trenchard's shirt, and when I came back, my sister, her hands full of strawberries, threw them, yellow glove and all, on the leaping pillars of fire. I shook the guttering candle out of its stick; my sister unscrewed her spray and emptied the precious stuff, that waved blue and white fingers at us out of the fierce, shrill yellow flames.

'So much for that,' I said. 'Where is he?' said my sister. We looked at each other.

'This is our fault,' we said. 'We must go over. If it starts here again when we're gone, God knows what we're to do.' Then she said:

'The loft's the place. It started there.'

Outside, the orchard was full of bird-conversation. Inside, in half an hour we were to give a birthday party. We ran through the gap in the hedge and into our side of the house, which had become again part of one house.

Inside it we expected to find one large, troubled man, upstairs collecting things. Instead there was quiet, a kind of dead quiet that came to meet us down the steep stair. The loft door was open. On the flight that led up to it he was lying, feet down, his head upon the sill; his head invisible, wrapped up in what looked like a piece of dark green cotton, dirty and torn. We dragged it off.

'Burn. Burn.' My sister said.

Some of it was in his mouth. We pulled it out. His tongue and mouth were stained. We slid him down to the foot of the flight and got water.

'Draw it fresh,' she said. And 'Keep it tight in your hand', for I wanted to drop the cloth, to pull it away, as if it were trying to wrap itself round me, to stick to me.

We threw water on him. ('Two shirts already; what an evening!' thought a bit of me.) By this time I had hold of the cloth like grim death, for it felt as though it was straining away in a wind that wasn't there. 'Gloves,' she said. We went into the loft. The skylight was open, and the cardboard box lay open and full. She put on the lid, and put it under her arm, and we left him on the stairs and made off again, across the orchard to the fire. It was dying down. The room stifling, the wood sulky with oil-black. My sister flung in the box, drenched it with the oil, and stiff grey smoke poured out on us. She tossed a match on it, and there was the grunt of an explosion, and, as we jumped back, the fire poured up again. I felt a smart in my hand, as if the cloth was raw between my fingers.

'It mustn't fly up the chimney,' she said. 'If it does, it will come back all over again.'

There was a box of cigars on the table. We turned them out, and thrust it in between the thin cedar boards and shut it up. Flung it into the fire wall and held it down. The box rose once or twice, bucked under the poker and the shovel.

Then we went back to Trenchard. He had come round, and was sitting at the foot of the loft stair.

'Everything's burned,' we said. 'Tell us what happened to you.'

'God knows,' he said. And then: 'I was stooping to get the box, and something flapped against the skylight. Blew in, I suppose, and the next thing I knew it had wrapped itself round my head and I couldn't get it off. I tore at it and I tried to get out. Then I couldn't bear it any more. It was winding itself tight. Then I must have passed out. But, oh God, it was the smell of it...'

Lettres Imaginaires

I

My Dear,
        I have learned that I cannot speak to you any more as
to my temporal lover. If I tried you would force me into sentiment
and special pleading. I might appeal to your pity. We have not
known each other very long, but I am assured that with you such
a demand would be a piece of ill-breeding.... There is an image
of you in my breast, and an image in the world. But truth does
not lie in these presentments.

Let us suppose then that you have a Pattern-laid-up-in-Heaven
waiting to touch my elbow as I write.

'Sir, you and I have loved', but that's not it.

'Sir, you and I must –'. I find it difficult to continue.

The business should be commonplace, but a bizarre streak
seems to accompany my lapse into passion. It has been a freakish
crucifixion – from a delicate approach, conventional as a harlequinade; for ten days we loved one another – as I thought with
some quality of passion. You assumed my nature, I took on yours.
The change of spiritual hats was no loss. No one knew. We were
too sure to need confidants. There was no one to forbid. Our
aptitude was perfect and our opportunity. Then one night we
arranged to meet, and you sent me a strange telegram. Two nights
later you came in late to our little restaurant and said: 'This won't
do. I smell burning.' Now I like fire. I looked at you and saw you
were Wyndham Lewis's drawing of the starry sky, a cold Titan,
a violent Intelligence. You were holding away from you a jewelled
image which was myself. Then I knew that friend I might be, or

100

mistress, but not lover. That dance was ended. Essentially you were 'through' with me and resentful. But I do not love like that. I will not have this sensuality and this friendship. I march to a better tune. I will not listen while you play both air and accompaniment with your heavy alternate hands.

Dear, I was tired that night. Couldn't you have been gentle with me? It was not lust that I wanted then, or philosophy, only peace. I sat opposite to you, 'tower of ivory, house of gold'. Your eyes narrowed. Then, with some ingratitude, you damned me for the vitality which had sustained you. Gallic realism? perhaps – your Latin analysis stripped the beauty you had enjoyed. I matched my wits with yours, answered your questions, parried your threats, folded myself in my sex, offered you a delicate candour.... You were not pleased. Then I saw that it was not a game. Throughout your analytical protests there was a recurrent note. I understood that I was target for some sacred male encounter with its own might. Scorn for me was to reanimate your virtue – assure you of something you had lost. But then I could not make the analysis. Your sneers were too effective as you held my image from you. Your brilliant eyes swept past mine, you spoke with your hands. Then, with some irrelevance, you said there was nothing to make me unhappy. I was a cocotte who had attempted your seduction.

Sadism? Well, yes. Innate need for violence, vulgarly called love of a row? In part. But there is an x in the equation. Not since Valentine....

It is too soon for this to have happened to me again. It is making me cry and quiver. I remember how by your Sussex fire you laid my head on your hands, and crossed the hands I clasped lest my virtue should escape you. My rings had bitten into my hands. Your eyes were dark and profound, heavy with peace. I would not have had you change yet to this pursuit of a truth whose 'chic' lies in its perversion.

All this in three weeks. You say: 'She will get over it.'

II

It was too soon, my dear, to be hurt again. That's my text for tonight. You should never have comforted me if you were going to submit me again to torture. All my life I have been accompanied by a ghostly pain. Lately it has become substantial, and I have recognized it in some absolute sense as cruelty. First there was Valentine, then you. You know how you found me – grey and sullen – wasted through too much knowledge. You knew what I had come to see.

There were your compassionate words, you've unsaid them. Can't you understand, you fool, that you've unsaid them?

Look here. You must not imagine that this is a complaint, a whining because a man has refused to love me. You are under no obligation to find immortality in my 'white and gold and red'. But I think that you should have made up your mind. Do you remember what you said – 'If there is any goodwill that can help you through this business, remember that you have it.' Within a month you faced me across Porfirio's table – my evil personified. What does it mean? You see I have the mind's curiosity to understand and incorporate. It sustains me, nearly all the time. You need not have loved me, though it would have been better that you should. But your voice is flaying me like the noise of a scythe on stone. Why should my vitality have moved this impulse in you? Through you it returned to me augmented. Did you hate it? Did you crave to diminish it yourself?

Love, dear love – how dare you speak to me of love?

III

You have said that you do not trust life, so why should you trust me who am, at best, one of the 'naughty stars'? And I imagined that I was to be your reconciliation.

From such divergence where could we have found a meeting-place for love? If I, 'the brother whom you have seen', could not enter your house, where will God come in? In my vanity I thought that where one went the other followed. Sir – you have undeceived me.

What did you call me? *'dangereuse'*, *'false'*, 'essentially outside truth'. Has that last phrase any meaning? To me, it is plain tripe. I can only tell my part of this adventure. Louis – there have been times, often before some humiliation profound as this, when I have known myself for an artificer in a better way of love than men practise in the world. That does not 'prove me base', but may prove me dangerous. Did I offer you too much freedom, too much passion? When I stripped myself of jealousy and possession, did I strip you of some armour you would not be without? You allow me words. I might talk with you on those matters till dawn. But love is not a conversation.

An adventure has been lost. We shall not be together again, and in love how can one have the adventure alone? You hardly admit the possibility. I said, 'I could make it damned good.' You answered: 'Damned it might be.'

Am I to go through all my life looking for the lover whose pace equals mine? Is it always illusion that turns me here and there, saying that I have found him in my perpetual error?

The pilgrim rescued the lady in the dewy wood. There, without explanation, he left her to face the Blatant Beast.

IV

Last night when you had gone with your friends I sat down on the floor among the nutshells and cigarette-ends, and cried at the fire. I was alone in my house, and you had all gone home, 'lover by lover'. I was left, out of your thought, out of your dance. Not one of you but Leila had thought to say that it had been a good party. An empty wine-bottle rolled across the floor and chinked against a syphon. It frightens me when inanimate things move about. It can be lonely here, past midnight, under the great shadows of this rood, not easy to leave the fire and mount the gallery stairs and slip into the icy bed. Before I decided to attempt it and take aspirin, I wondered if this fire which you have lit – and will not share – has an 'absolute' value, a good-in-itself apart from you – and from me. Eventually one takes the way from one's kind.

This afternoon I went out in the rain and through the streets, not faint with desolation but in tranquillity, with my love.

Pathological?

Later.

I am waiting for you now. Will it be the same if you do not come? How can it be, when my eyes are starved, my quivering touch cannot fasten. I want our old ritual. I want to play it – to satiety. Don't you remember you would sit by the fire? We'd be alone. I would sit on the chair-arm behind you. You lay there, silent, relaxed, as life flowed from me to you. Did you know what I said as I kissed your neck – that I laid my peace on you – the peace you've not had? 'My peace, not as the world giveth....' Your astonishment made me laugh. I slipped from the arm on to your knee, and crossed my feet, and swung there. I can see you laugh. I can see your quarrel with life remembered to be forgotten.

'Oh, my dear, you happened, but just in time, only just in time.'

And I believed it. My eyes went hot because of the miracle. I used to watch the flush on your thin face, the sudden fusion....

You used to laugh. 'Was there ever woman said such things before? Witty fool!' I would slip from your knees on to the floor and crouch there, looking up at you, silent.

Then it was your turn.

You are not coming tonight. I was mistaken. There is no adventure alone.

V

Half an hour later – a knock. External shapes, the walls, the coloured glass on the dark shelf, became like scenery, flat, two-dimensioned. Crossing from the fireplace to the door, I knew how my body bent as though the great chair had risen and clung to my back. You were not there, but a boy with onions. It happened again. I said: 'It is not Louis – it is not.'

It wasn't. I saw a girl with a suitcase and umbrella and several kinds of fur – a girl you have not met. She wanted a bed for the night. The sequence was amusing.

That evening we compared our beauties on the floor, by the fire on the white rug, burnished our nails and our hair. Our scents and orange-sticks lay between our feet – my long pink toes and her short ones.

She threw down her mirror. She must speak.

She had gathered – indeed she knew. I had given myself – and to more than one man. I was not married at all. I did not seem to mind. Did I know what I was doing? I was giving men what they wanted... I exacted nothing in return. Did I know the 'awful degradation' that was overtaking me? No one could be more passionate than she – but never. Her fiancé would come back from the front and kill her. (There's a chance for Ivan.) She was proud to think that she would come to him. Just all of her – (Price sixpence. Please see that this seal is unbroken.) Incidentally, she considered me a blackleg in a pair of silk stockings...

She has left me to wonder, though – without passion – whether you, Louis, are despising me. (She does not know about you.)

You have called me pure. Do you still think that? Did you ever think it – with your mind? I don't care. If love of truth can make me pure, I'll pass. And so, what woman cares a pin about chastity? She tried to frighten me, damn her.

Then later I saw her puny man, and lunched afterwards with Bill, and drank with him, and comforted him in sexless amity; and then came to me, as there has always come, the answer to her fear.

VI

Well, my dear. We've had it out? I repeat if it had been another woman, lovelier, wittier than I – Dolores, Bill's wife, or some other *amoureuse* – you would be dead now, spitted on a dagger. Or the lady would have hung herself on your door-knocker, leaving you to explain. You are not grateful for my moderation. Yet you behaved rather well. You were skilful. I watched you manœuvring to reduce our affair to the terms of the harlequinade. When you explained that you were not worthy of my least regard I grasped the setting and gave you your Columbine. What did it amount to? That I, who had brought you peace, had become the devourer of peace. There was no greed of which you might accuse me, but you made your case against a vitality which might destroy.

'It is my deepest opinion that a philosopher must avoid love. I cannot – though I have wished to – recognize your life of intuitions corrected by intelligence. It interferes with pure mentality.' And then: 'Dear, I have wanted to – I wish I were different. But I mean to draw back before I hurt you any more. It is intolerably disagreeable to see you suffer.' Your eyes pleaded for my departure. I stood before your mirror, colouring my mouth. In that glass I saw your magical presentment. In it was mirrored the boy scientist, the 'Varsity philosopher, the emotional adolescent. Heaven's hound called herself off. I left Soho, and you, and the tragic-eyed woman I passed on the stairs. I was almost at peace, on the edge of contemplation. I did not cry when I reached home.

I am become a dawn-cat, pattering back with torn ears and fur. A month ago there seemed no beauty my body could not accomplish. Loved One, there is a great gulf outside formal time between our Sussex days and these.

'When the Lord turned again the Captivity of Sion.'

Sion has gone back into her Captivity – 'credit me,' as Stephen Bird would say.

It's all right, Louis – you are not my lover. You are a boy, and have sharpened your senses on the scent of my skin and the colour of my hair.

As a lover you are nothing. But the truth of your presentment does not lie there. I've found it. This also is true. Herein lies your originality. Most minds in the world are cheap, sterile, insincere. They impart their stale flavour to the whole. But I have tasted your mind's fruitfulness and passion like salt and fine bread. There is your way, your truth, and your life. And I have lived with you.

VII

Today we met – almost as strangers. We both wished to resolve our affair into formal acquaintance. We finished a bottle of Burgundy. Old Porfirio, who had watched this and other of our affairs, was pleased to see us. He had noticed that M'sieu came no longer with the tall Mademoiselle. There is a gentleman tucked away behind that round stomach. Do you realize that he is not licensed to sell liqueurs?

We walked down Drury Lane greasy with banana-skins, and

you held my arm and spoke of Anne, that 'wafer made out of the blood of Christ.' I could not point out the ritual error while you were telling me of her trust, explaining that her confidence appalled while it elated you.

O sacred *naïveté*! Has it never occurred to you that I have behaved to you in exactly the same way?

That's as may be. I could have sneered, till I looked up and saw your face. You might have been a flame enclosed in ivory. You were thinking?

To you: Endymion, is it all one moon who in the innumerable phases of women turns to kiss you? Adolescent, sensualist – are all women alike to you in the dark?

We walked under the portico of Drury Lane.

Khovanchina – I do not understand the full implication of that music, except that it united us for a moment, to separate us, I think, forever.

When we came out the Great Bear trailed over Covent Garden, and the empty pavement rang, and the stars leapt in the bitter sky. The music had ravished and troubled me, but your cold elation gave me the fear of an animal that knows it is to be beaten. 'It's all there,' you said, 'in that last Act. The negation of your passion – your pleasure, and your despair. There is the end of being, voluntarily to become nothing, to evade – courteously – your angel of the adventure. Withdrawal, stillness, immaculate contemplation – there is escape with victory. Isn't that better than your daring and your temperance?'

We came to your door, went upstairs without speaking. You did a strange thing. You came beside me, music in your eyes – and on your lips. Then, your eyes closed, you flung yourself down upon my breast, and clung there.

I held you, sitting upright, dazed. Then I heard Jim on the stairs. He came in and found us very quiet. I went home.

You're a brave man, Louis. I cannot accept final futility, Dostoevsky's bath-house full of spiders, the ultimate rat in the ultimate trap. You are a great man. I 'also have known a lot of men', but have not met one before of such intelligence.

You can put them away – things which feed you: Mozart and Chekhov and Plotinus, ballet and *décor*, your physics which only vaguely impress me, your economics with which I do not agree. You can put them away and bank on the ultimate bankruptcy of all cognition and passion. I love you, I adore your quality. I'm too proud to fight.

Varya

VIII

> How am I fallen from myself
> For a long time now
> I have not seen the Prince of Chang in my dreams.

Today I went out on the word of a lying map to look for hut circles and kist vaens in the mist. I believed also that there would be ghosts on the moor. I found those I had brought with me, awaiting me there. The mist filtered down and covered the world. I wandered over those soggy uplands, and listened to the silence made audible by running water and the odd settling noises of the bog.

It was not the stone age that pressed round me, but my metropolitan ghosts. I found them translated in that iron land whose focus is a prison and a house of torture. The images that haunt me – the horror in Valentine, the shadow of the war, the starvation of the human spirit, the thwarting of creation, the power whose symbol we call cruelty, rose out of the moor, ghastly familiar. When the sun strikes it after rain it is the colour of raw flesh. Find me the greatest common measure of these things.

IX

You asked me once: 'What can I give you that other men cannot? My intelligence – perhaps – but not my person, or my wealth – I am hardly a sexual athlete.' And then the demure smile, and the stroke of the moustache. Dear fool. Am I to accuse you of idealizing me? Don't you know that there is a sensuality in me no one has ever satisfied? I'm tired of echoing Aspasia and Egeria, but with you I've been romp and *amoureuse*, shared the 'ardours demi-virginal' of the Kirchner Girl.

We've had the profundity of infinite lightness. With you I've danced my solo in that equivocal ballet of the world.

X

Prince of Chang – I think of your pale face and high cheek-bones, your narrow brilliant eyes, and you seem to me remote as that Prince. You might be an enamelled lord, and I once an embroidered lady, two pieces of *décor* in an age and city remote as Atlantis.

I have now been a week on these moors.

> Great London where the sights are
> And the lights are
> And the nights are.

The memory of our affair is not dead, but it has become a magical *objet d'art* like some awful tale of India or Japan where the raw blood beats through porcelain and cloisonné and jade. What has Ivan made of this? Nothing. I haven't told him. I'm learning to offer myself in instalments. Besides, it won't make a tale yet, and to cry the raw pain aloud would not be fair. It is not his dance or his crucifixion. It is hardly his business. But I cannot give him what I would. I've been too starved. There are better ways. All the time the moor watches me and the granite hills. The cold streams hiss between the boulders, the mist is soft as thistledown and cold as death.

There are better ways than this acceptance of mutilation. We are creatures in time, Ivan and I. Years have knit us, of love and adventure. He is my temporal stability. But we three together? The moor is destroying me. Here nature and the Beast – Sologub's Beast – are one. The moor is a repetition of the war. The town is a microcosm of the moor, stripped of its grotesque beauty. I am a tiny seed in such a mill. There are better ways. When he and I first sat by the fire, I remembered you, Prince of Chang. There is a *pas de trois* in love, two cannot dance.... Another way of saying that I don't see why I should not have you both. The result of the frustration is that I am bored. I sit here, sucking smoke up a tortoiseshell tube. The taste of you burns my memory – like the vile cigarettes of this abominable place.

XI

Dear Brutus,

I am in town again – with more humour than when I left it. At least I watch the completion of our cycle without further illusion. It is like this. Since Sion has gone back into her captivity, she will drink freely of the waters of Babylon. My dear – you don't know – women who can stand this can stand anything. I do not know what absolute value it may have, but I remember the night when the thread was cut that tied me to temporal needs. I have lived in a world become translucent. But I cannot gauge the quality of the illumination beyond. My feet have been lighter on the streets than on the day you said that you loved me. Then I strode through them, part of the combers of the wind and the hurrying stars. My bird had left the bush and dropped into my hands. Now there is neither bush nor bird but a stillness like sea-fog. I am relaxed, passive. Then I remember. 'For God's sake don't stop loving me. I have everything to learn. Make my world new.' And then: 'You have come in time, only just in time –' and the tears force themselves out of my eyes, separate as stones, and each a microcosm of my disappointment. But the worst you've done is not these. All that I might have written, all that I might have perceived, the adventure I saw and have not accomplished – these I can present you. You begot them. You aborted them. Now I am barren. That's the worst you've done.

> 'Complaints are many and various,
> And my feet are cold,' said Aquarius.

There is your side to this tale, and I, perhaps, be none than a green-sick girl.

Last night in your rooms, I could not but laugh. You were so glad to think that you had steered your canoe safe back to interested acquaintance once more. Dear Brutus, there was nothing to forgive.

Varya

XII

Faint white world,
I stand at my door.

There is' snow on every plane of the street and over them a mist, an ice-gauze. There is nothing more. I can live without you and without any man. Yes – 'Be sorry for your childishness,' and dance again and run about the world. Nothing more. Not for you. The air is an unshaken silver net. It hangs in suspense outside of time. So with me.

Remember the last act of *Khovanchina*. I do not know whether I am alive or dead, but that there is another state through the antithesis of life and death. There is a cloister for passion. You by denying, I by acceptance, have come to the same place. But there are no final vows. O Tranquillity. There are no more grey-walled houses set to watch us or conceal, or scarlet buses grinding up the Tottenham Court Road. There are only masses and spears of light, coloured, interchangeable. All things are dissolved into their elements, all things dance.

Athis....

In Bayswater

'Some passages in the life of an only son'

I

He found the road behind Westbourne Grove where there was the cream and laurel-green cottage where he wanted to live. He had heard that it was to let and was persuaded that it would be cheap, because of the neighbourhood, because there was no Tube, because of the Portobello Road. A woman made of dirt-stiffened rag was its caretaker. She told him a fantastic rent. He had begun to live in the cottage years before. In the last resort, he liked to wound himself observing his own piteousness.

He crossed the ivory boards in his muddy shoes. There was clear yellow paint inside and a round window over the porch, set in deep wood. He put his elbows in it and listened to the wind in the poplars and thought that he was in an old, resting ship. If four shared it, it might be possible. He had not four on whom he could rely. A clean laurel grew in the back yard. He picked a yellow leaf and wrote on it and put it inside his shirt. The great window at the back was made in small panes. He wished he had a diamond in a ring to cut his longing on it. The kitchen was flagged. The larder had a marble shelf for cooling and in summer the butter would not run or the milk sour. There was a glass and white wood cupboard, and shelves for books.

'It is nice,' he said to the woman, 'but there is no geyser in the bathroom.' He knew that she knew that he could not pay the rent. He thought, how, if he took it and could not pay, a life of beastly evasion would begin and corrupt the still beauty. He had no nerve to dodge bills, the technique of frightening him had been too

developed. He went out, the leaf pricking him, and forgot to give
the woman her tip, so that the wretchedness might be completed
by a bad exit, and the shilling still be there for tea.

The round window followed him that was the house's eye, a
ship's window, the shape for the eye of the wind. Small, square
windows are good, and wide plate sheets, well, he could not have
them and must go back to the sort that rattle and stick, that look
out on mean arrangements and illuminate them.

These are the fancies of a man looking for a house. His next
was the Portobello Road because of its crime. It was a fair walk,
as Londoners count it, into a hollow full of bright shops, a market
and a crowd, a moving, merry place. There were squat glass
pillars full of sweets, called cushions, of the texture of silk. There
were little pieces of meat classified and no carcasses. The poor
like thick gold watch-chains, and little earrings stuck on cards.
He pretended to be envious, while he had no sense of it at all.
He imagined a freedom, but the rich vitality, the bestiality, the
arrangement of wit, innocence, and corruption had no relation
to his nature.

He wanted his tea.

The leaf had made a small sore. He pulled it out. On the yellow
underleaf was a red line he had scrawled: *From the house with the
round window we are kept out of,* and his name, *Alec.* The letter
was broken by the veins of the leaf. He put it away. He did not
notice the people who had noticed him unbuttoning his shirt. He
walked away to the right into a district of tall houses whose doors
stood high above the streets at the top of high steps. Some had
pillars. The dogs ran along lifting their legs against the high,
frayed area rods. The road also ran up.

Into a city of charwomen. They climbed out of deep areas.
Soon he saw they were everywhere, descending, rising, in their
rhythm; young in glazed cotton furs, mature and very pregnant,
old with scum in their eyes. Rooms would be cheap and include
the services of one of them, and that would make a gesture.

Rain began. Wetted at dusk, the streets' patina of filth gleamed
like stale fish, and out of the crests of the houses came noises of
weeping that never was, that never could be comforted. A stiff
old gentleman with white whiskers and a red face let himself into
a boarding-house with a long bright key. Alec saw him and

remembered that the family of a man he knew lived in one of these streets, and that his friend used to live with them. If he called, there might be tea, and he liked the idea of contact with the man again. He filled a coloured disc in Alec's mind, violet and blue with little gold flecks. He looked up and saw the street. At the first number there was a brown visiting card with the man's name under a bell that did not ring. With his lips against his fingers Alec called up the tube. His breath beaded its mouth and moved a clot of grit. A woman let him in. He went up the high stairs that smelt of dust. At the top of the stairs he found their flat, the door flush with the step. He was half-enchanted, saying *these are not natural*, forgetting he had come for human contacts and tea. A little old woman opened the door, dressed in dull silk, and a small coat of black wool over it. Her wedding ring was of bright gold and very thin like her hands. For an instant she peered at him and then began to smile.

'Come in; you're a friend of Charles, I expect. I'm afraid he's not in, but he may be back.' He was drawn inside, and separated from his hat and stick. A tall, sullen, pretty girl left the room at once to make him tea.

'You see,' she was saying, 'I am Charles' mother, and that makes it so difficult. How can I say anything against my own son? But sometimes I must...before my daughter comes back. A girl's innocence should be respected. Once it's gone, it's gone for ever, as Landor says.... But he drinks, my dear boy – you'll forgive a short acquaintance and an old woman, I know. He drinks, and stays out half the night – all night, and I don't know what his journalism brings in, but he gives me nothing....'

It had been going on some time, and the impact of the idea, substituted for his idea of Charles was like the pricking of the leaf. He took it out of his pocket and split it down the back. So a generous man like Charles was a cad to his mother. – What was she saying?

'He says he is fond of his sister, but he does nothing for her that a brother should do. He brings men to the house who ignore her. He says she is not smart enough. He sneers at her. There is something in him all the time that makes me afraid.'

Rubbish. What did she mean by that? This was not interesting.

It was mean. As Rutherford he stood for charm, as Charles he was becoming wicked, just simply wicked like a man who starves his dogs, and also obliquely, medically wicked, responsible and irresponsible, a double treasure for the connoisseur.

'I am so glad you came. I like to meet his friends. Charles tells them I am a spiteful old woman. But I am all alone, and I have to keep it from the girl.'

Why? Poor old thing. I don't suppose she has to.

'We all thought him a good fellow. He is our authority on periods and *décor*.' That ought to please her – mothers like to swank.

He wanted to hear more, and was beginning to be ashamed. He did not attend to the shame, and was arranging a fresh cast when the girl came back into the room, staring contemptuously over the tray. He took it from her. She blushed and scowled. There was bread and margarine and with them a superb cake.

The delicate voice spoke like a gramophone, round and round, to no one.

'My daughter is a good sister, she loves her brother Charles.'

'Don't, Mother.'

'Why not, my dear? Wasn't it only last week that you replaced the eyeglass he is always breaking? I know it cost ten shillings, and on your salary.... I tell you about this, Alec, I knew that you were the one Charles calls Alec as soon as I saw you, because of what you said about his being an authority on dress. Oh, my dear boy, if you saw his room, the filthy state in which he keeps his things, his rubbishy novels, his ukalele that makes such a wicked noise, I think; the cigarette holes in his sheets. I know I am a nervous old woman, but some day there will be a fire, and he will burn to death and we're very fond of him, all the same, aren't we, dear?'

'Mother!'

'But, Mrs Rutherford, what does he do that you don't like?' He wanted his appetite quickly glutted.

'Charles...I can't bear to go into it...' She paused and winked: 'I must leave you and see about dinner. Charwomen can't cook, and I'm determined that my children shall have one good meal a day. Charles...'

He was left alone with the girl. A more abstract part of him had already sketched a mask from her pale bold face, and hot ignorant eyes.

'Your brother Charles...'

'You must not take my mother too seriously. She does not quite understand about young people. Charles...'

He thought: You are ten years younger than he, you silly maid. You want smacking. And he said:

'Yes, I agree, but what does Charles really do?' He rearranged himself, raking back his beautiful gilt hair.

'Charles drinks – he leads a bad life, whatever that is.'

'We would admit nothing, but that he is sometimes drunk.'

'There was a night here once – anyhow he thinks dreadfully. He told me to read a poem once about a bad woman. Mother was frightened – I know too that he is friends with a woman who is not married and who has a child. He would not tell us that it was not his child.' Alec thought: But this is ordinary rubbish. I'm wasting my time. Good advice, and I'll go. He said:

'You should try and be matey with him then. You should go out with him, make him show you people. He might not drink so much if you were sympathetic. Nothing is so beastly as when brother and sister aren't friends?'

'Mother would not hear of it. You don't understand.'

'What don't I understand –' – I'm off, but I did say the only thing that's always true when I told her to be matey.

The girl went on: 'Charles does not think that one can do anything wrong. I don't understand these things. I never go out except to work. It is lonely.'

He forgot the stiff lines of the mask he had made of her, lost himself in psychology, and psychology in pity.

'Well, now I know that Charles has a sister, perhaps your mother will trust me.' This is going it – I am off home. 'Make my apologies to your mother, I have an appointment.'

'What did you come here for?'

'I've been looking for a flat.'

'There is one to let on the floor below. We have the keys. Mother, let us show him over the flat below.'

The mother came out of the kitchen. 'Do you like apple dumplings. I hope you'll stay to supper and only hope Charles will come in. I've kept my hand for pastry.' She led him affectionately downstairs.

The flat was frightful, a low room with jumping panes and

sprawling flowers and yellowing paint. A hot blue bedroom. From the streets he had fallen into domestic anguish, and into rooms that were the interior version of the streets' unrest; and though the retreat was open, he was not sure of it, because the old woman was a witch and would diddle him, the girl her apprentice, and Charles their conjuration. He saw Charles as a stone idol that walked. He was damned if he would take the place.

'Charles. Charles. Charles.'

Someone was coming upstairs. To his active ear the slow step sounded deliberate. Here was Charles coming, who did not think anything wrong, who was cruel to his sister. Who would not take his sister out. Who had an old woman cooking for him upstairs. Whom Alec knew as another person. He was out of the door and after him.

Charles marched past him, did not look at him. He followed him, feeling kicked, up the black stairs. He saw the girl beside him suck in her mouth, and then a frail call: 'Charles, my dear boy, here's a friend you'll be glad to see. Alec whom you've told me about so often. He is staying to supper,' and lower, 'You will be nice to him, won't you?'

They crowded on each other into the little room.

'What in hell does he want?' asked Charles. 'I'm going up to my room to be sick.'

'Have you no respect, Charles, for my drawing-room?'

'None.'

His sister screamed. 'I can't bear it. I can't bear it.'

'What can't you bear?'

'We were having tea with your friend, and showing him the flat, and it was nice and amusing, and you can come in and shame us.'

'And what would you do if I didn't? Exploit me till there was no telling which was your son and which was your husband, eh, ma?'

Drunk – dangerous. Might be sick.

'Rutherford, hadn't you better come up to bed at once?'

'In the absence of that woman's spouse, I am head of this house –

My fathers drew the righteous sword
For Scotland and her claims,
Among the loyal gentlemen

> *And chief of ancient names,...*
> *Like a leal, old Scottish cavalier.*

In Bayswater we have other occupations.'

He had taken the hearth-rug position, his arms open, grasping each end, working his olive neck. They waited. 'Charles, why do you mind us knowing your friend?'

'Alec, I must apologise for these people. This is why I don't bring people home. I am as drunk as drunk, and where's some food?'

'In the kitchen. I'll bring it up to your room if you're going to be sick.'

'I'm not going to be sick. Is there anything to drink?'

'You know –'

'I know there is going to be some. Go out and get it, girl, and we'll play *pass the keystone.*'

'Give her some money, Charles.'

'Damn her, why should I?' The girl went out. Alec rushed after her.

'Go back, my dear. I'll see to it. You must let me. I insist. It is abominable.' This is not possible. He sings: *His golden locks time has to silver turned.*

In the street Alec shouldered people left and right, ran into the wine shop and out again with the sour drink.

When he got upstairs, the women were talking low in the kitchen, and up and down the tiny sitting-room Charles was pacing, talking, striking at the air. An ugly boil showed above his collar, a patch of skin on the heel above his shoe. Alec noticed that a great ring was gone from his elegant yellow hand.

He stood in the doorway, licking his mouth. Then he said: 'Here's the keystone,' and then: 'I say, Rutherford, wouldn't you be better in bed?'

'How long have you been here?'

'About an hour.'

'What's she been telling you?'

'I never knew you drank like this.'

'Turn it into a nice mime, man. That's your job, isn't it? What did she say? Tell me, or I'll wring your neck.'

'She minds your drinking. What mother would not?'

'Go on.'

'Oh, and the way you keep your room; you've got such a flair for beauty, you know.'

'Good man, you've told me, now I'll kill her.' He spun Alec out, lifted him, dropped him, hitting the ground with him, and went into the kitchen. There were screams. Alec rushed in. Mrs Rutherford was sucking her hand. Charles was leaning against the dresser, tears falling down his face. He spoke first:

'It is finished. I am going up to bed.' He went out on a light swing, and as lightly up the bare attic stairs.

'This is too awful. Mrs Rutherford I am going to take the flat below. I may be able to help you. I could come up at a sound. You are all alone here.'

'Bless you, dear boy, bless you.'

He was just conscious that this was the sort of good deed to be done quickly. He ate her dinner, he went out to telephone, he slept on the sofa. The women whispering in their bedroom were quiet. He sat over the fire. There had been no sound from Rutherford's room since his door had shut. Suddenly his mother in a red dressing-gown came into the room and sat down by Alec.

'Dear boy. What an entertainment for you. Must I tell you that it might have been worse? Poor, poor, poor son of mine. To think of his singing like that. You know we really are people of that sort. The last poor ghosts of a great family. May I have a cigarette?'

She sat slim and straight, head back, hand up, like a boy. Alec saw the boy. He saw the room and its implications. He thought he saw the possibility of romantic adventures. He saw his retreat closing. He acquiesced.

II

One of the charwomen was creeping about his bedroom. Alec stood about the living-room afraid to touch anything lest the dirt-scum should rub off before the woman had given it a semblance. He could feel her revolving slowly, on an unfresh, quiet morning, when his mouth was sore and his body dazed, with only the sleep interval between him and the dreadful stories upstairs. What a family – compact of malicious and sexual crime, tragic lives and comic deaths. He remembered a great-aunt who had had twins, who had crawled to her husband's bed and left the bodies there, and had hung herself from the chandelier, and her toes tapping the foot of the bed had waked her husband in the morning.

... The girl would leave the room with her irrelevant hauteur and the mother's voice would drop to a hiss and out would drop a toad and Charles would improve on it. *Putting the jewel in the toad's head.* Phew. There could be a series: Bayswater nights.

The flat was horrible. He slept at one and two and three, and woke at nine and ten and eleven, and often went out without washing, rehearsed, idled, ate too little, ate too much, till late night, like a black madness, drove him back. Not to study, talk, and imagination, but to a dogged run up the black, smelling stairs. There he found them, not often Charles, not always the girl, but always the old woman, and a series of obscene, absorbing stories. The flowers he brought them withered in the vases, the classics they borrowed were not read, and it seemed to him that if he took them away it would make a position clear of which he was afraid. He was on a tide and felt it, with reprobation, with amazement, with anguish, curiosity and fear.

The mother fed him, and he sometimes cooked for her, but she would not learn his dishes though she praised them. There was always praise. Instead of a small clean green house and some pretty bits of furniture, praise.

Charles, since that night, had been charming. He had not come there often. He kept his disc in Alec's imagination, night-blue, spangled with gold; and another arrangement where he might murder his mother, and terrify his sister, and refuse to explain why.... He was in a circle by himself. Alec heard his soft bitter voice, whose sound was lost in the mother's reiteration of praise.

'Charm, my dear boy, of course he has charm. All my husband's people have charm. He reminds me of poor Lord Byron.'

'Where has he gone, Mrs Rutherford?'

'Oh, to his room to work, I hope.'

Alec thought it must be cold up there with the stars shaking over it.

'He drove Mrs Sumner out of it this morning. What a state it must be in. You are so particular, Alec. I like to see that in a young man. There is an uncle on his father's side —'

Alec felt for the cigarette he had long ceased to enjoy. It was the first time she had got down later than a grand-parent. It had been saga as much as scandal. She had said 'uncle'. That might mean that they were coming to the history of living beings, not death-gilt heroes and heroines he had dressed in their costumes as she had moved them naked in their sins.

She had a husband 'away at his work and shortly to return.' She was preparing him.

'His uncle Raasay won't speak to us.'

'Because of Charles?'

'Because of something that happened before Charles was born.' Among the various properties of Uncle Stewart's career had been a collection of obscene books. 'He was like Charles about his bedroom, and when he died they were found. I sometimes think that Charles may have something up there.'

Charles knew any number of amusing things that had happened about cod-pieces and beds and medicines and make-up and songs.

'Of course you must not think that I mind the classics – I don't think it's a book, but he locks the door, and if he'd only trust me a little – Do you know what he said to me when I asked him?'

'I heard him tell his sister she had a mind one could make toast at –'

'He said *to the filthy all things are filthy* staring at me with that ridiculous eyeglass. An eyeglass with the clothes he wears.' She fretted on.

In the afternoon of the next day he was alone with the flesh-raw flowers, and when he had thought of blood and flaying and Assyria, and the uncommunicative shapes of cuneiform, he had backed to the door, and stood rattling the handle and let himself out and then went upstairs. There was no one in. He pretended that Rutherford might be in, and for the first time went up his stair. His door was not locked. Alec's conscience went on squeaking like a ghost.

The room was stirring in the thin wind.

There was a pale stone Buddha, an iron bed with a red blanket, and a night table with a marble top, and a blue quicksilver ball. A nice set. He saw these and began to look for something to see.

It takes time to look at books. There was a basket-handled sword. No fireplace. The servant's room. Pink toothbrush. Did his mouth bleed? A chest of drawers the colour of mustard to write at and dress. A piece of silk on the wall in Charles's colours. The wine-dark. If he finds me here, I came up to borrow a book. The devil take him. He never told me he had these....

He squatted down on the boards.

There were all the Italian writers and portfolios of fallen columns and standing columns and well-heads whose contemplation should occupy a gentleman's leisure. There was a Boccaccio, on parchment, the page spaced with small witty cuts. Alec turned over on his face, and an hour later, put them away with guilty accuracy, and went downstairs.

If there was a secret, it was hidden. He had not believed in it, only hoped for it as he might hope for a drink. He left the women alone that night, and the night after Charles came down to his rooms, and a friend came and another, and they sang, but Charles would not sing, and Alec fancied he might be going to cry, and put off telling him that he had gone up to his room, because one confidence might force another. He knew now that everything would happen in its time, and this was the root of his perception, the excuse for his weakness, and made him a happy man.

The next night they were not cordial and he hardly noticed it. The night after he was making a stage-model and there was a sharp knock and he had let in the girl, sulky and liquid-voiced and fresh from tears.

He noticed that he would like to force her into a corner of the room, twisting her arms and supposed that one or both must be in a high state of erotic excitement.

'I'm not supposed to come,' she said, and scowled, then, with a prepared vulgarity that scandalized him: 'You won't let on to ma, now, will you?'

He wanted to say: 'My dear, it is quite proper for you to spend an evening with me and I shall not make a mystery about it,' and felt again that mixture of disgust and vital interest, when she fell down into his armchair and began to shiver without crying, so that he could only say: 'What is it?' and at his gesture, she exclaimed: 'What must you think of me?'

He looked down into the hot eyes, at acting become obscene through excess of lying, but at raw hunger. It was personal and impersonal. It was the impersonal that interested him. Her race was boiling there. She ought to be singing, not squirming there like a typist, singing another bit of that infernal saga that was coming up-to-date, that was coming up-to-date.

Poor ravenous kid. She should be given flowers and kisses and taken to bed. *Cover her with flowers.*

'I'm glad you've come – listen to this.' He went to the piano and sang the pretty song, and played some Mozart to sensitize and detach himself. When he joined her she was bolt upright and sneering:

'What a good chaperone a piano makes.'

'What is this fuss about propriety? It is awfully silly.'

'I was only thinking that we need more than a piano upstairs. That's why I came. That's why I came.' She said it the first time with sober tragedy, the second time like a caress.

'Has Charles been unkind to you again?'

'Oh, là, là. Don't let's go into that. Please, Alec. Yes. Yes. He sneers at me. Oh, God, why aren't I dead?' He thought: I'll get the truth out of that girl if I wring her beastly neck:

'Now, look here, tell me the truth.'

'Yes, Alec, I will. He sang a dreadful song about – I can't tell you, but you can guess, and when mother told him to stop and he wouldn't, I ran into the kitchen, and he followed me in there still singing.'

'Now, mind you tell me the real truth.'

'He frightened me. I ran downstairs.'

'You must explain it more. You haven't told me anything to believe.'

'I can't, I can't. Oh, comfort me, comfort me.'

They're all mad. I must start from that. They're all mad. His brutal temper is making the girl neurotic. Poor little beast. Is it a trick to get hold of me? No. No. Charles is off his dot – I needn't be careful – it's awful. 'My dear –'

'Alec, it's silly to mind, but when I minded he snatched my little seed-pearl bird out of my frock and threw it out of the window. It was very old, and I haven't any ornaments.'

Alec found he was beginning to cry, and, when he checked himself, the sense of danger rose behind the pity and interrogation and balanced him. He was leaning over her staring when Charles came into the room.

'What have you been doing to the child? How dare you throw her bird out of the window?'

Charles took no notice and said to her, 'I want to talk to Alec, wouldn't you be better upstairs?'

Alec, expecting heroics, saw her face swell into a puffed, white, whimpering mask.

'Rutherford, you leave that girl alone. She came down here with a horrible story I don't believe.'

'Believe it man. It will have truth enough to suit you.'

'Until I know it's a lie, I must protect her. Nothing upstairs makes me believe anything but that you are all mad, but she is too young to tell nothing but lies.'

Charles frowned: 'Will you listen if I tell you the truth?'

'You said that her truth should satisfy me. Suppose it does?'

'So?'

The girl turned in her chair. He thought of a dachshund lying on its side.

'Sit up.' She sat up immediately, a young gentlewoman.

'It is good of you to take care of me.'

'Look out,' said Charles laughing.

'Man, how dare you laugh when you have driven the child so crazed, she doesn't know what she's doing or saying?'

'Alec,' said Charles, 'are your intentions honourable?'

'God, man! Are yours?'

'What are my intentions? They are to leave this place tomorrow morning, and my mother can try my father for a change.'

Alec was just going to ask Charles humbly for the truth, when the girl began to wriggle and chatter, bolt upright in her chair, turning her body from one to the other.

'Charles, please, please go away. This is the only refuge I have. It hasn't been all fun being shut up with mother. Alec, you know I came down…I was afraid it was wrong, but I came because it was quiet, and you would let me cry. Oh, Charles, you might give me a chance. I will tell Alec all the truth.'

The men felt that they were acting in a story from a magazine, the present race-fable. They saw each other. 'You go to bed,' they said.

It was not easy to get rid of her.

'I hate Mother as much as you. Let me stay with you. Show

me, and I'll be the kind of girl you like. Give me a chance. I ought to have a chance. You are my brother.'

'I agree there,' said Alec, and immediately the image of another kind of living was clear to him and he said:

'I wanted to live in a small green and white house that was quiet with a tree, and a round window and stones on its floor. I came here instead without wanting to. That was mad. Without being mad I have lived in an asylum I am going to rationalise for myself. I give in to it. I do not understand what you are all about. But I'm going to.'

Mrs Rutherford slipped into the room.

'My dear, what are you doing here? I am very surprised. Alec, what is my daughter doing here? She's not a bohemian, to be in a young man's room.'

Alec and Charles each noticed the other was feeling sick.

'I followed Charles down to get my brooch.'

'What brooch?' said Charles.

'My brooch he threw out into the yard.'

'It will never be found,' said the old woman, 'you had better go upstairs.'

'It does not exist,' said Charles.

'Something exists,' said Alec, and then: 'Charles, what have they done to you?'

'It is time,' said Charles.

The old woman said: 'Haven't you done enough for one night? If you will excuse me, I will take my daughter to bed.'

Charles said without violence or pleasure: 'Would it surprise you to hear, Alec, that I have just come in?'

'There is rain on your shoulder,' said Alec. 'You have just come in.'

'Then I could hardly have been bullying my sister. At present I have no hat.'

'Stay here with your friend, Charles. I did not know about this. I will get as nice a supper as I can, and call you both.'

Charles fell into his sister's place in the chair by the fire. Alec said: 'I smell burning.' He did not move. They both said: 'It is nothing,' but Alec ran out of the room, mad with the feeling that he must be there first, and up the chocolate stair he would see history making, saga-history, the drama and the psychology caught for a moment in the event, the historiê.

Upstairs in an iron tray on the kitchen floor Charles's *Decameron* was burning to death. There was the white core, curled edges that glowed and went out, brittle metallic pieces lifted in the draught to the four corners of the room. The cover his mother and sister had torn off lay on the table like a sham. Their mutilation had left a block of sheets, too well-sewn to come apart, whose lit edges had gone out. Many loose sheets were burned away. The book was dead.

He did not hear them following. He stood about.

Poor Charles. His treasure. This was what they did when there was no one looking. He was convinced at once and became Charles's man. He wanted to put it all away, just to hide it, then to bury it. He burnt his fingers on the tray.

'Charles,' he cried over the bannisters: 'Charles. Come and see what they've done.' Charles came.

'There they are,' he said, 'now do you see?'

'Yes,' said Alec. 'I mean I don't quite, but I want you to forgive me. Let me do something. Oh, your book, your book!'

'It is the way they relieve themselves,' said Charles. 'She is malignant against the pleasant things, and the kid is mad with thwarted instinct. That's what they do.'

'What can I do for you?'

'Nothing.'

'For God's sake don't say that.'

'I didn't like the way you came in here. You told them, I don't doubt, that I was the devil of a fellow.'

'You know them. It was like going on falling.'

'All right.'

'I'd better tell you. I sneaked up one day to your room and read there because they said –'

'That there was something obscene there.'

'No. I did not tell them.'

'Are you keen on my sister? Why did you stay?'

'No. I was interested. At first I was really taken in. Then –'

'When my mother over-did it –'

'I felt that I was in a current – I wanted to find out the truth. I was inside the houses of these streets. It is the opposite of my values. I wanted to get through this way into what *is*. Living with demons made me a cad. I am begging your pardon. I will pack and go.'

'And leave my mother responsible for the flat and rent.'

'What am I to do? I'd beat the girl and wring the old woman's neck.'

'It is time to shuffle the cards. You might stay and see what we can do.'

Alec felt beaten, forgiven, blessed.

'They're still here,' he said.

'Coming in too,' said Charles. 'It is more than a stanza, it's a canto. I'm glad you see it like that.' He guided them in and pointed to the floor.

'That is what you have done to my book.'

'If I were you, I would be ashamed to have such a book for a girl to read.'

'How did she come to read it? She sped up to my room at your orders.'

'You must have left it about. I found her hysterical.'

'So did Alec. Stop it, Mother. You have overdone yourself this time. It was also a valuable book. I had meant to sell it and have given her the money. However, she amused herself with it another way.

'Why couldn't you have laughed at it? It is a jolly book. You've got its sheets for domestic uses.'

'Alec, would you allow your sister to read it?'

'I should be ashamed of her if she couldn't.'

'Come,' said Charles. 'I am going to bed. I am going away tomorrow. Perhaps, Alec, you can give me a bed for the night.'

'They have all left me but you.'

'You have my sister.'

'A girl. You are the head of the house.'

'While my father lives?'

The girl wailed: 'Alec, persuade him sometime to forgive me.' He went across to comfort her, and when he put her through the door he heard Charles saying:

'Prospero burned his book: they burned mine: my book is burned: they could not bite, they hid the tooth: they could not see, they stole the eye. I am starving. I am blind.'

Alec's heart climbed up his throat; he took Rutherford away.

He remembered the streets, three weeks back, where there was weeping going on that never was, that never could, be comforted. He would like to have had the girl, too, and run all night from one to the other, and patronise one while he worshipped the other. He felt sickly and refreshed himself, remembering that he was finding out a truth.

He saw Charles undress, feebly, dropping his clothes for him to pick up and fold, gaily, silently.

He said: 'It's a pity we've no drink.'

'Have you any tea – China tea?'

'Yes. My mother sends it to me. She is kind –'

'Tar and jasmine. Make some.'

He fell into his bed and lay flat, smoking. Alec came back.

'It's been going on for two years. Since I came back sick. I thought they might give me a roof. I meant to shape the girl. I heard a bolt snick. I was curious too. There is a great smooth tide we call a rost. I was drawn on it.

'I don't know why it happens. Why the old sow eats her farrow. Why the farrows are eaten. I couldn't make the girl see, though there's not much difference between a paralysed rabbit and a paralysed fox.

'She's not omnipotent either.'

'Why didn't you quit?'

'Fatigue. They are wretchedly poor.'

'But, tell me. I heard you speak brutally to them.'

'Oh, man, when there is nothing but untruth, one must *make* a reality, or become one of the lies. Any reality will do. It is a quality that one famishes for.

'I made myself part of what she said, to give her truth, which stops madness, which is release for her and for the girl. I am a man of my race, I want truth. Universal truth if I can get it, anyhow particular truth. Even my décor I hitch on. More tea. But she won on me. I am brutalized, gelded, spoilt.'

'Listen to me,' said Alec. 'I have got some cash. We are going to take that house.'

'What house?'

'My house with the round window, the dear place.'

'I should improve it. I tell you I'm next door to mad. I even need food.'

'You'll have it. You must let me do it for my own sake.'

'All right. I used to have a will. I suppose one can recover even from a mother. You know, I have a terror that one can't. I am very sick tonight. My God, what harm had the book done them that they must destroy it – the clean page. When I was a boy she gave us things to break, she was a scolding housewife that soiled things in secret with grease.

'She told me the great poems were filthy. "I am guarding you against yourselves." *An exile I have washed me clean.*'

'Peace,' said Alec. 'We'll do better by our own children.'

'I've lost my faith in truth. I'll leave no children. I'll do my bit to end the world.'

Alec devoted his life to him.

'This persecution is over for you now. Don't you know that? Do you hear?'

Rutherford tore away the clothes and began to toss.

'They murder, they are murderers –'

'We're at an end,' said Alec, 'that is sure. At the end of a set of evils. Slowly, one after another, they're going to be eaten. There won't be any left.'

'You mean,' said Charles, settling down in the easy bed, 'there is going to be destroyed *all things but beauty alone?*'

And Alec, to whom beauty must be mixed with love, slept beside him.

III

It had been Alec's intention to take Charles away, but next morning he found him occupied and disagreeable, inert in every part but his body. Alec was shy and took his cue, accustomed by life to these disappointments. He had an idea of paradise that was a state uninterrupted by breaks in fortunate continuity. Upstairs it would be quiet for a time. He did not know what the mother and the sister would do, but they would find a way out for themselves. Man must do that, and those people always do. The worst of men do the most impossible things, have to do the most terrible things. *God is not mocked.* He winced that he could still think like that.

He loathed his occupations till they relieved him. By the

evening he was tranquil enough to say: 'There will be an empty week. Perhaps a week and a week. *A time and a time and half a time.* We shall begin again. These Scots families carry Scripture with them. There is the father to come back.'

He passed the girl on the stairs with her head up, slowly stepping. He wished her an illegitimate baby and went off.

Two nights later a little old man hopped upstairs in a dreadful hurry. Alec was afraid that it was not time for life to become again a condition of music, but went about his room remembering what that condition is.

And Charles was not interested.

'Pa's back,' he said. He called him that always, with a spit, and 'ma' with a contempt that masked hunger.

Alec could not bear it and took him out to dinner, and with friendly cunning gave him all the drink he wanted, letting him choose and suggested 'tell me about your father.' Charles, glowing at a red velvet bench, refused.

In the street Alec said: 'I think I shall walk home,' and Charles said: 'Do you mind if I come with you?' and in Holland Walk Charles sang.

First he sang:

> *'My father is a clergyman, a good and honest man,*
> *My mother is a Methodist, so I do the best I ca-a-an.'*

'You said he was a schoolmaster.'

'No, he was a priest.'

'Oh,' said Alec, excited at the Roman mystery, 'how did he get out of it?'

'He left a note on the vestry pin-cushion, after he had celebrated mass, that he had lost his faith. But it was because he loved my mother. He has never lost his faith.'

'How has he combined the two?'

'Not at all.'

'But what has he done?'

'Perhaps he maternalizes her. He has been the great cuckoo squalling in our nest.'

'And the cuckold?'

'I expect so. She hates him now.'

Then he would talk of nothing but of some discoveries made

in Etruria, but he talked so well that Alec's mind sprang wide and he gave him his attention, keeping the rich morsel of story to enjoy alone. Charles had brought a camp-bed and placed it along the opposite wall at the foot of Alec's, and slept there, neat and formal, chilling his host.

Alec saw the father next day running up the stairs with a bunch of flowers. He was like a greying dog, and by no means, in himself, a formidable man. Alec gave up the effort 'de se taire' and began again observations that would end in spying on matters that spying would not illuminate. In his life he had known too much ill-luck to believe in good luck, but still felt that it might be induced. When his sitting-room door did not shut easily, he left it open. When a friend came, he held him in talk on the stairs. Charles was out all day, came in late and sober, asked politely for his bed, slept in it folded like his figure on its tomb; did his share of the breakfast, ate it and left the house. But on the fourth day he asked for his father. He was restless for a little, and said 'I must see my father.' He went into the bedroom, and drew a comb that smelt of sweet oil through his black hair, and went over his face with a little wad filled with brown powder.

Alec, who made up well, in the theatre, never did more than wash and whip a wet comb through his magnificent hair. He feared that he would not be able to go upstairs again. A saga is not heard by inference. He was sad, and was careful not to examine the point of anguish behind the disappointment – the sense that he and Charles had nothing in common...

Before he had expected him, Charles came down.

'How did you find him?'

'Not so bad. There are times when I quite like him. My mother improves when he first comes home.'

Alec was disappointed till he had tasted this.

'My mother gives him such a time. He still thinks her incomparable, like an infatuate with a mistress he condemns and can't live without. Not that he condemns her. He only wishes they were both angels before God. Oh, how he wishes this business of living over, and so do I, and so do all our house.'

'I don't see that,' said Alec. 'I still like things, green leaves and frisking and the good hearts of friends.'

'No,' said Charles. 'I want Venetian palaces, which, once and for all, are not to be had, and cannot be won.'

'While your mother is the worst housekeeper I ever met. She can't make a pattern of plates on a dresser-shelf.' This annoyed Charles, and Alec was not sorry. His irresponsiveness had bruised him.

My little son, do not take sides in a family quarrel. My mother's advice. Damn the old ladies. They knew things.

When he got home that evening, he found a little blue note that Charles's mother would be so pleased if he would come up and meet her husband, he was very solitary and so liked young people. Alec's going upstairs was like the passage of a nightmare, slow, and swift in extreme opposites, and he was not himself when he pushed in the door, but a stuttering greed for sensation of which he was no longer connoisseur but glutton. He grinned at the bowed backs about the fire.

The girl would not turn round, or look up. He thought he would tell Charles that when she was old she would be a nasty woman, and remembered that no one knew that better than Charles, and that Charles must not think that he talked clichés....

Charles was showing off a point of erudition.

The old man listened with respect. Alec listened, fidgetted, had no comment. He was crying to himself that this was a Volsung house, and they should be singing. Charles's ivory stick in the corner by the fire was the sacred tree.

But they didn't grow round Charles. Yes, in a way they did. Alec did not see exactly how. But he would have liked to hear them sing.

The old man said: 'Don't you think, Charles, it would be very interesting to have an article on Byzantine monasticism in the new quarterly? I'd rely on you a good deal.'

The girl said: 'Do you remember the wonderful dance you took me to when you wore the gold dress and the curled purple beard?' and Charles said: 'Yes, and you wouldn't stay out of pure, sullen refusal to play –'

'I had warned her, Charles, that it was not a proper place for her, but I don't doubt you'd find her more broad-minded, or shall I say more corrupted, now? But here is Alec. I'm so glad to see him again. Didn't I tell you, Father, all he has done to cheer an old woman up?'

'Do you know, Alec, she has broken the most horrible silence about the dance? What truth is there in them?' Alec felt readmitted....

The old man began to fidget. He did not look directly at his wife and daughter, but obliquely at the men. Alec said: *he was once a priest.* An operation of magic was done to him: if he had eyes, he has seen something outside the course of nature. I say that it depended on his eyes. They say that it did not depend upon his eyes. He has heard confessions. He has elevated the host and censed it and given extreme unction and called Mary an ivory tower and exorcised ghosts. Here he is with wife and children. He has done too much.

The old man belonged to the majority who do not approve – say of cats or earrings or bus tickets. He tried to get a denigration out of Alec, who could not think of one. He was wondering at him and trying to remember a piece of theology, when Charles began to give his father a piece of his mind.

'I tell you, people ruin their lives trying to mean both sides of a question as both sides. You can mean a question one way or another, or as many as you damn well care to invent; but you are not to mean two opposites at once. Of course you can mean them if you do not think of them as opposites. You can mean *everything.* But you have to know what everything is, don't you know...'

So Rutherford was drunk. A good beginning for the night. Alec began to ask him to come to bed.

'I want Father to see what I mean.'

'I see that you are drunk, sir, and in your mother's drawing-room. I have known since you were born that you would come to no good end. You say that you can make no money, that I never gave you a profession. Your mother needs a winter coat. Look at your collection of books –'

Charles spat into the fire and sat rigid, while Alec's heart beat.

– 'I do all that my circumstances warrant. My son should supply my deficiencies. I am a much ill-used man, and mother, mother, – she is not kind to me.'

His voice ran up. Alec stared and shrugged to himself. Rutherford flung his arms round his mother's neck. 'We understand one another, the old lady and I. Don't we, ma?'

Alec knew that the gears had been changed, and the engine

that had balked would now climb. He blew his nose and looked over the crest of his handkerchief. Charles and his father might be going to cry, no common tears. The old lady had unwound a small roll of braids, tacked on blue paper, and began to knot some dirty threads. Alec cocked his head. That was a web. She was making lace. She makes lace when her men are beginning to cry. The girl looked as though froth would bubble out of her heavy mouth. He lost his sweet feeling for Charles. Charles was part of a play. Not even protagonist. He had no time to feel ashamed. Sometimes love is restored to the quiet soul that Alec wished to have and that his simplicity encouraged and prevented.

Would the song never begin? It did not begin. They bickered. Then Mrs Rutherford said: 'Why should he sell his things when you could give me a coat if you cared to. If you had kept your post in that secular school, we should have been well-off. There's a man for you, worrying about his soul and not his wife – not even about his pretty daughter.'

'Don't, Mother.'

'There are times when I must speak out. Do you know, Alec, that whilst she was being born, four old priests sat outside our house, in a cab, cursing her as she made her first cry, and me for bearing her to a man who had been one of their priests. Isn't it like them, the shaved men!'

This was reward. There are rewards and fairies. Was this in fairy land? Certainly not. 'You must not make those curses real,' he cried and was not noticed.

'It is she makes them real,' the old man cried.

Alec wanted to hide his face....

Mrs Rutherford and her daughter went to bed. Alec recognized that brightness in the air which marks the appearance of a form of life to which man is not unusually sensitive. His mother would have said: *There is magic about.* The father and son discussed projects and literature. Gradually they began to move. One looked for cigarettes behind a photograph, the other for matches, for a hand-kerchief, for a suitable piece of coal. In the cramped rooms they swelled, and round Alec grew shadows that met on the small ceiling, drove into one another, mixed, and moved out. The son said:

'I shall go and see if Mother is all right,' and the father: 'I want to ask the girl something.' The women slept together. The men did not go. Alec saw the women laid out like saints in neat iron beds, the old woman thinking, the young woman feeling. Nasty, ill-educated girl. No. Charles's sister was capable of thought....

Charles was not drunk enough? How much would it cost to make Charles drunk enough – drunk to ecstasy, not drunk to witless braggings, drunk to possession by the dark daimon?

Outside the miseries were streaming up through the roofs, the constant incense that did not even smell nice. It was not much of an exchange for the old man for the sweet scents of his altar. He remembered a barrow of cherries fresh with rain outside a Paris church. His innocent cocky youth made a face at him and dropped its mask. Misery – Miserere. – There was no lord. We are not allowed to believe in a lord any more. There is a great prince in our hearts. Rutherford knows that and I, he and only I, and for that we are lié'd for ever: But that prince is in prison. I take him out when I can, and Rutherford shuts him in. I want the salvation of Rutherford's soul. Do I mean anything when I say it like that?

The salvation of his soul means that the prince has come out for ever. A thing that has never happened in the world.

Alec left them moving about and went downstairs to bed.

Charles came in to breakfast and said that he had spent the night wrangling, and had then gone for a walk in the pale morning rain. He added: 'Are you sure that you do not mind if I stay here, because the old man is getting ready to turn me out of what he calls the house?'

Alec said that he could stay for ever, but that it seemed strange because his father had asked for his opinion on several important matters and had listened with attention. 'You will see,' said Charles. Alec went out to work. Observation had become a creation like a piece of needlework to be picked up, added to, and perhaps be finished.

A few days later Charles said: 'I have made a great mistake – I wanted a recommendation from an old friend of pa's, and I asked him to get it for me. He promised, but he warned the man not to give it.'

'And what will that cost you?'

'A great deal, I am afraid. It was for an excavator's job in South Italy. I shall not go now.'

'Oh, Charles, it is insupportable.'

'It is,' said Charles. 'I sink and it lies on top of me. How dirty one feels when one says: "I am doing my suffering".'

Alec saw that it was a small, beastly tragedy. Charles could do that work, it fed his imagination and would feed his body. It would lead him back to consideration, honour, luxury. He thought that Charles must have these in order to be himself. The old man had lain in ambush for this. Alec hated him and tried to be rude to him, but he went on looking peaceful and wretched, fussing about the rooms, never leaving his wife, still asking his son questions. His son answered patiently until, two evenings later, he went up to his father and said:

'You are trying to ruin my life and you still pick my brains, you wicked old man. The sooner you die the better.'

Alec had expected something more from Charles than this commonplace. It was a little better when he added: 'In spite of you I will live and do the work I like. My mother and my sister can starve. They are your job' – and the old man skipped with rage and said nothing. Alec laughed, too, when Charles added: 'I will not accept your responsibility,' because he articulated like a good Scot.

The girl opened a rosy mouth and sang:

> *'Charlie is my darling, darling, darling,*
> *Charlie is my darling*
> *The young –'*

'Blackguard,' shouted the old man.

'Hit someone your own size,' said Charles, lifting his noble height, and above his laughter, Alec watched and could make nothing of his eyes.

'You will never come into this house again.'

'Do you challenge me? I am going out now and my last state will be worse than my first.'

Alec followed him out. 'You've done it, this time, Charles.' He made him no answer – Alec wanted to catch at his sleeve and was afraid. Only a woman could do that. He had to stop a sob of excitement, pain and humiliation. Then he thought that Charles was going out to drink and had he enough money to get as drunk as he wanted to get? He crumpled a ten-shilling note into his hand. It was taken without recognition. Alec went into his sitting-room and left the door ajar. Not for an hour. Before midnight, Charles, who had fallen in the road before a 'bus, was carried up, they presumed to die, and laid on his mother's bed. There was a dry hole where Alec's heart should have been. He helped them that night, and, when the doctor said that Charles did not seem intoxicated, went out on to the stairs and cried and thanked God. He wanted to help more and went back, and from the living room he heard the girl crying in hysteria, and her mother controlling her with great sense. The doctor was in the kitchen. He went to the bedroom door. Charles was on the bed, black and white and young, and by his side his father stood, in exaltation, his hand lifted, absolving his son; and, as Alec saw, absolving himself also, not from past malevolence, but from carnal generation and from women. Alec also saw the father exulting in the son, and afraid that he would see what was being done to him, and that Charles had seen, and was curious, angry and amused.

Just then the mother came back, past Alec, into the room and spoke cheerfully: 'My son is not going to die.'

IV

After his parents thought that Charles was as good as dead, Alec did not leave the affair alone. Independent of his preferences he had an eye for truth, he was preoccupied with Charles. He knew that Charles wore masks. If Alec could not unmask him, there was trouble about that might strip him. He was not afraid that anything common would be exposed. If he had thought that, he might have been afraid and gone away because he was looking for something that was greater than life. Instead, in sensual fever, he evoked pain on this man, ready to stage him and weep over him at once.

After his accident he took Charles away into the country and talked to him about his complexes, his father's complexes, his mother's complexes. He was invaluably silly to Charles. There was an idol once taken round Scandinavia in a cart. He went about through the villages with Alec. He did not tell him anything.

Alec decided to find Charles a woman, a girl of parts to play baggage. He brought Charles back to his people's flat, his visual mask red-gold that had been yellow-gold. Alec explained that he could not find the money to take another place; probably Charles insisted. They lived again in the pagoda, Charles on top, then Alec, and a creeping woman in the basement. She cleaned for Charles's mother, and the old lady sat on the dresser and they would talk. Alec's contact with the district was over. He had described it to his friends. Over the street there was a set of empty rooms. In league with Charles's mother he let them to a white girl called Billy.

The flat was damp. Her furniture came tied up with ribbons. She went about like a blooming, fresh toadstool on its stalk. From the first Alec lost interest in her, but his instinct for treachery made him bring her upstairs to see what the old woman would make of her. They made it a favour to have her, she made it a favour to go. She asked for a footstool. The easy tea-party became formal, a duologue between the old woman and the young. The girl hated her, deep in her sullen pool. Alec was bored. Charles had bruised him. He could take the girl or leave her. He might take her since his people disliked her. Billy rose to go. She engaged the party to return, dropped a little veil half-way down her face, and went down to her flat. She put on a dirty dress. Her eyes set into grey glass beads. She lay with her hair in a fish skeleton the cat had left by the fire.

Alec went away for a short tour. He came back into a windy, violent spell of spring, and found about one quarter of his flat occupied by a young man. He said that Charles had put him there and had paid the rent. He was called Festus.

'He wrote to you for permission, but the address was lost. I will go at once if I'm in your way.' Alec's sentimentality was not vulgar; his weakness, by which he meant to inherit the earth, was also kind.

'Of course not, my dear boy. You must stay of course.' He was not sorry even when Charles came in looking like a tree trying not to put out a leaf.

'Festus was homeless between the jobs.'

'I gave in and did what Charles told me.'

After tea Festus washed up.

'Hard, bright and sweet,' said Charles at the slight, elastic back and drew in the ashes with his stick. 'I am very fond of him.'

'How long have you known him?'

'A long time. He rationalizes his affection for me.'

'I can see he adores you.' The small change chinked in Alec's pocket. He had set the stage and he was not to play. He saw a young saint and an old saint walking in a paradise that was a cold hillside.

This was something that Charles had found for himself. Charles was warm. There was a deadlier cold about. He felt himself run upon icy sticks.

'Is he as mad as the rest of us?'

'Yes.'

'Only adolescence I suppose?'

'He is formed for his age and very intelligent. But you must be right. By the way, Alec, why did you bring that girl, Billy, here? Mother is saying that she won't know your cast-off mistresses. Festus would like to save me from her and I can't gratify him –'

'Your mother wanted the place let –' He was pierced and weary; 'I can't please everybody. If you keep a tenement, you try and let it. I see what unites you and Festus. Some new humbug about sex. I'm sorry you don't like Billy. I'm off to look her up.'

'I hardly know her.'

At the door he turned back to see Charles lie back and smile at Festus as he brought in the dish-cloth to dry it at the fire.

Billy let him in, yawning inattention. Billy at home was new. He sniffed about. On a table representing a mushroom there was her photograph in chiffon and a rose. Stuck on the frame there was an abominable portrait of her in orange-peel and buttons. She showed it to him. 'Festus did that.'

'Did he give it to you?'

'No, Charles.'

Really. She did not see that it was not kindly meant. What fun. He readjusted.

'How is life getting along?'

'I'm waiting for my contract to go to Los Angeles. It is all settled. The director is taking me over with his wife –'

'Or as his wife?'

'I wouldn't think of such a thing. I'm getting my clothes –'

Swank of the métier. Why try it on me? We all starve together.

Play up. 'How many people are dying of love for you, Billy?'

'I'm tired of love. A little quiet spinsterhood suits me at the moment –'

Pale hands I loved. Dear – dear. He thought of a piece of white, smooth, dead wood.

'Sergius wants me to marry him and go to Russia. I might.'

'But you're married already.'

'Only technically, after all. The Soviet would divorce us.'

Lord, the vanity of these fancy-girls.

She began to be eager.

'Do you know, Alec, if I had not been brought up a Catholic, I should like to be a Buddhist. What do you think I'd better do?'

'Be a Buddhist.'

'I can't get over what I've been taught. A clairvoyant told me that I was once the wife of a Samurai. A man no one can see follows me about. What do you think of reincarnation? I haven't seen him for a long time.'

'Seen who?'

'My spirit-husband. Some day he will materialize and give me everything I want.'

'Why not? I want to get this life over, you know. It's dull.'

'I'm surprised to hear you say that.' This ass I tried to foist on Charles. I must tell him this.

'He comes when any danger threatens me. He tells me what I am to read. Once I was staying in a house when a murder was done and I saw him. I don't know why I am telling you this, Alec.'

Nor I. 'Have you seen him lately – since you came here?'

'Not at all. Your friend Charles would be sufficient to keep away any real psychic manifestation –'

'You don't like Charles?'

'He seems to be simply negligible, that's all.'

'And Festus?'

'He seems a nice boy. It's a pity he's so neurotic.'

'What's his trouble?'

'Oh, he imagines it is his duty to kill himself. Didn't Charles tell you? I imagine it was Charles put the idea into his head. He is just the sort of man to suggest morbidities and give them a greater value than normal facts. Festus has had a hard life. He has told me all about it. His father was a brute –'

'It sounds a plain doctor's case. But he mustn't die. Charles wants him.'

'I can't see that Charles ought to be considered. His life is spoilt already. Can't you see he is rotting where he stands.'

Alec wanted to bounce. Wanted to box her ears and smack her behind. Charles had not told him everything and she'd guessed. She had asked him in to say what she had said about Charles. She had poured dirty water on Charles. She had a spirit-husband. That bright, righteous lad was going to die. Charles would be so upset. Oh, dear. They could not have it to themselves because Billy was here. Billy at other people's houses. Billy drunk, Billy sober, Billy broke, Billy amorous, Billy-by-the-fire. Two men called to see her. Alec was sent to fetch more cups. Two boys with a car. Festus was not that kind of boy. One of them took his chair. Billy was standing up. Beasts. He went away.

Charles was rotting. He saw Festus out of doors, giving Charles blood out of a spoon.

'She says you're no good, Charles, my Charles.'

'Follow up,' said Alec. 'Let it be quick, let it be quick, my God.' It had happened quickly. He had left Charles to his darling and gone off with Billy. She was always ready to talk about them, but he left it to her. He asked her to interfere, to consult Charles about Festus, but this she always refused. For reasons she would not give, for no reason, because Alec did not understand, because Charles was responsible, because no one could approve of Charles.

Alec said to himself, 'Charles does not come to me. I am entitled to find out what Charles is like.' Then he discovered that Billy saw Festus, and was doing her duty on behalf of him. 'He spent yesterday evening with me, and I've found out all about it.'

'No one has told me yet,' said Alec, 'why he should be killing himself at all.'

'He thinks that he is fated to kill his father,' and this from Billy seemed enough, because Billy did not understand pride, innocence and torment. He could not think of a better answer. Festus had gone to lodge in another house.

One day Alec was coming in quietly, he heard Charles talking to Billy in her room. After the first interest and inhibition of listening, he listened. A high voice and a low noise. The acute interest went out. He was irritated and knocked at the door. They did not say 'Come in' at once. He went away.

Billy said: 'That was Alec. We'd better ask him down.'

'He will find out what he wants without our telling.'

'He might think that there was something between us. Will you fetch him?' Charles looked at her and then, slowly, did what he was told. Alec would not come. 'Tell me yourself.'

'Festus is going to commit suicide.'

'Can I help you?'

'I don't know.'

'Are you trying Billy?'

'Alec, will you take Billy away?'

'No. How can I? She doesn't count. Why do you want that?'

'For the sake of the clean issue.'

'I don't think, Charles, you are quite the man to manage a young suicide.' Charles sighed. Alec went on: 'Why don't you take him away yourself? And you mustn't be jealous of him.'

Charles giggled.

– 'From the look of you I should say you could do with a change. Can't you leave town?'

'I don't want to at present.' Charles went away.

Alec began to shiver. It was then he prayed for it to come soon and suffered because he had deliberately offered Charles sense.

Charles had earned sense:

He went down the stairs after him.

'I'm sorry you're troubled. Please let me be of use.' Billy said: 'Festus has gone out by himself. I think we ought to follow him.'

They went out. Billy in a purple coat, Alec in grey, Charles in black. Through the dull spring streets and the grit-laced air they hurried to Festus' lodgings. He was not there. 'I know where he sits.' Charles walked them to Holland Avenue. It was getting dark. They walked on the right side under the trees. 'There he is.' Alec saw a dark boy upright, alone on a bench. He looked at Charles. Billy said: 'I suppose I had better go. He ought not to be left.' He wanted to push Charles on and hold him back. She left them instantly. 'Not her,' he said to Charles, but she was sitting on the bench, a black cap the back of a white neck, and purple shoulders sloping.

'It is your place and all you'll do is to save it up against her that she took it.'

'The pubs are open,' said Charles.

When they got home, they called on Billy. 'It's all right,' she said. 'I've got him to promise that if I'll help him to do it later, he'll put it off for three months. It's a bargain. But he must have company.'

'We'll all keep him company. Good for you, Billy. Now I must be told why he wants to do it all.'

Charles said: 'He is going to do it because he believes he can never express in himself his idea of excellence.'

'But we none of us can. Why can't he see that. Why should he want to? The vanity.'

Billy said: 'I said I would go round at eleven to his rooms. I'll tell you everything in the morning –'

Alec was dazed. His mind would not focus.

There was a tightness and a white blur. He felt he must strangle or be strangled.

'Is she doing her best d'you think, Charles?' he asked, as they went upstairs.

'The pubs aren't shut,' said Charles.

They sat in the saloon.

'Aren't you letting Billy have all the responsibility? Can you trust her? I wouldn't. You won't like it if anything goes wrong.'

'I am enjoying myself so much up to the present.'

'Why do you let Billy act for you?'

'My hands are tied,' said Charles.

'They're not, they're not,' Alec shrieked. 'Use your great wisdom.'

'I have none. Let the female do her part.'

'You're afraid of the responsibility.'

'I am *not* afraid of you or Billy or myself. Believe me, Alec, in the past I did everything that suggested itself to me. Now we are on an ideal plane, and I have no ideal solution.'

'Ideal plane! Can't you see it's an adolescent neurosis?'

'Believe me, it is like that now, and nothing less. Let the flesh do its bit.'

Alec did not think of Billy as flesh. Charles frightened him. Charles was playing up. He squirmed.

'You'll be in an awful state.' And what state am I in throwing silly fits before my friend in his necessity? When it's over, I'll help.

They did not go to Festus' lodgings because Billy would be there.

Next morning Alec woke up feeling sick. Billy was about, very brilliant.

'I've sent up a note to his mother to let Charles sleep, whether the charwoman wants to do his room or not. Go round and call on Festus.'

'Won't you come?' She was uncertain.

'No, I must get my place straight. I've left everything because of that boy. I should like to –'

He could not bear to stand about. He went.

He found Festus dead in his bed. He sat down beside him, feeling very cold.

Get the news to Charles. I have to do that. Thank God the girl didn't get here first. She mustn't see him. So that's what he took. I must find the landlady. *In any case you leave a body behind you. Such want of method.* Can we persuade them it's accidental? We must try. Charles would wish that. I must see about…

But he walked out into the street, and, at the impact of the air, he swam and drank it.

Festus is dead. Charles knows it, but he has to be told. How unfair.

I'll tell Billy and she can tell Charles. That's a frightful idea.

'I've got to tell everybody. I found the body. Who killed cock-robin? It's quite all right. I hardly knew him.

'Take Billy down a peg. Petty cat. Suppose Charles says nothing. If Charles doesn't come off it –'

Come off it, you bitch. Leave us men alone. The pretty dead. People go mad and die to illustrate Charles. The illustrated life of Charles. He tore along: with a thick throat shouted up to Billy on the doorstep: 'Festus is dead.'

She flung out her arms, and strained her palms on the door

frame and opened her mouth. She stretched back her head and then led him in.

'Had I better tell Charles?'

'No,' shouted Alec, 'you go and tell the landlady, tell the police, tell the postman. I am going to Charles.'

On the stairs he met the charwoman.

'There's a glove, sir, from one of the gentlemen who was here last night.' A huge motor-gauntlet like a dead animal.

'None of us. What gentleman?' Suppose Charles should come downstairs.

'Last night, sir, a gentleman called. Before eleven it was. I heard him with his car. One of Miss Seton's young gentlemen. He took her for a ride in his car and they didn't get home till it was nearly two, I heard them.'

'Give it her.'

'Oh, oh, oh.' He sat on a stair. We left him to her. He asked her to go. She said she would go. She did not go. He killed himself.

And well the car Love guideth.

Follow up.

He walked firmly upstairs, straight in and up to Charles' room. Charles was awake, propped up, his elbows tucked in to his sides.

'Charles. Festus is dead. He took poison last night. I found him. Billy did not go to him as she said she would. She went out in a car.'

'Dead is he,' said Charles, and threw himself out of bed, into an overcoat and went out past Alec. 'You can tell my people.'

Alec told them and went out after him. There was no Billy. Beside Festus' body, Charles was giving directions to the landlady and the police. He gave Alec telegrams written out to send. They worked all day without speaking to each other.

They had the inquest and buried him, received his family and sent them away. They ran it between them. After two days' absence Billy went about among them again. When they could not repeat the story, she told it. Eventually she did all the telling. She invented a mysterious silence when the men began to talk about their affairs again. Then she left the flat and went away.

Alec followed Charles about. It seemed to him that Charles carried a quiver of shafts when a shot meant salvation.

Brightness falls from the air. It had fallen when Festus died.

He wanted an arrow to stick. He followed Charles up to his room. Charles had offered a contact like brushed velvet. Alec wanted a kick or a blow. Charles sat up against the wall. Alec, sitting, reached across the table to him.

'Do for God's sake tell me, Charles. Do you understand about Billy?' he cried at him. 'Did she know what she was doing when she left him that night? Did she want it to happen? Yes, want it to happen? I can say it now. It's a good thing she's gone. What does your mother say? You must admit, Charles, I've been reasonable and asked no question?'

Approfondir the business for me, for pity's sake.

'Aren't we friends enough for that?

'Stop playing the velvet cat. You've played it since that morning. Can't you see you're being too proud to show your broken heart? But I know it's broken. You might occasionally come off it with me. I'm not in training for hero. I've been helping you bury your friend, and a ghastly week it's been. I'm going off for the weekend. I wish we could go together.'

Charles listened to this. Alec became ashamed and stopped. He had exposed himself to Charles. Perhaps all this had happened that he might be lured on. Like a split plum he was lying in Charles' mouth to be spat out. Excess of shame squared him against Charles. Charles said:

'Let us take Billy first. There is a common girl, detached from the preoccupation of her class-type, and who dares not be bored. Her ennui was like a vacuum, into which everything was sucked.

'You brought her here. You have an uncritical reliance on the female principle. After the example underneath us. You have not got the key of the mothers.

'I suppose you thought that Billy would satisfy your curiosity, but not as a rival. She cancelled out with my mother, but that was no gain for she was unready for fresh action.

'I was asleep with Festus. You got tired of Billy. I'm not her size. There was Festus like a thin rod incapable of evasion or compromise or the least adaptation, stripping a male reality, and you two around clapping your female disks.'

We laughed.

'Then Festus' little obsession came to a crisis –'

'What was it?' Alec muttered.

'A simplicity. He had stripped certain aspects of virtue and when he found that he could not exactly reproduce them in his daily life, he decided that he was not fit to live, and must immediately die.

'There was also a boy who was better than he was at his job.

'I made the mother's circle till you came along and charged the air with that blonde bitch. A young man does not do it easily. She got going. He died as easily as falling off a log.

'They were getting on quite nicely you remember. She was busy saving and pushing us gently away. He was full of gratitude and simplicity. He felt he would not die, and wondered how I could have been so right without knowing her. She withdrew and he instantly died. And there rushed into her vacuum intoxication, orgasm, flesh for dreams. She will feed on that for a time. She will be something for a time. And that's that.

'These were your arrangements, Alec, to enlarge your theory of me; to illustrate, explain me, punish me. The developments took their own line. When I could not act, I stood out. Now you are shocked, but you will find that you have gratified your nature. You will not describe its instinct to betray, you will only feed it.

'I betrayed you when I practised my feminine element on you. Superficially you sentimentalized yourself into pique, into indifference, but your instinct found Billy. She has done the job for you. My boy is dead. My mother will be stimulated.'

'I can't stand any more,' said Alec. 'Kick me, kill me' –

'Or cry to you. That's your sensuality, but I'm not under the obligation. I am on exhibition here before you, but I give my own show –'

Alec took out his pocket-knife and sawed the blade into the hard blend of his wrist.

The blood and the good pain saved his reason.

'You are right, you have given your own show. I see myself. I am your slave. I will go away for ever and become not your slave. Some time I shall be at peace and not your slave. I mean I understand and thank you for this explanation, for your show. I'm going off because you'd be justified in treading me in like a slug – you'll feel better if you know you'll never see me again –'

'By no means,' said Charles.

Widdershins

E very day he woke to the desire to take the world by the throat, and choke it. He had no illusion that the world wanted to be saved; still less that it was ready to be saved by him. Ready! – it was punching at him with agonizing blows, to be rid of him, once and for all. He woke up. Even that was not true now. It had been true once, but now the world was getting over any slight alarm he might have caused it. It was leaving him alone, to realize the wounds it had given him. Sometimes it was even tolerant and trying to patch him up.

Oh, God!

He was in the middle of London, in a dull hotel bedroom, stale with travelling from the Shap moors, where two years before he had gone away to think. He had called it thinking, but he had gone there to lick his wounds and dream. He was just intelligent enough to notice that he had not thought, and that what he remembered was certain moments of action. Certainly he did not understand that what he wanted was magic.

He lay, and remembered something about himself: that he was called Dick Tressider, that he was a mystic; and that among the people he met the word meant a snub, a cliché, an insult, or, very occasionally, a distinction: that he knew a great many people who almost realized his plan, and yet did not: that he was a gentleman. He had not thought of that for a long time. London had reminded him. He damned the place and ordered his bath. He shaved, and put on his good, worn, country clothes, his heavy boots, his rain-coat and leather gloves, all without pride in his strength, or tonic from his unconventionality. He ate a country breakfast, and looked up his appointments. He felt that he was held from behind

148

by the short hair on his skull, and cursed the city. But what he needed was magic.

It is doubtful if he understood the idea of progress, but whether he did or not, he disliked it. It may be certain, but it is obviously slow. He had his immediate reasons too. He had tried every association which tries to speed man's progress; labour and revolution, agriculture and religion. In each, it was the soundest point in his perception, he had seen one thing and the same thing, which was the essential thing and, at the same time, did not come off. Meanwhile, labour and revolution, agriculture and religion were entirely sick of him. He knew, if any man living knew he knew, that sometimes things were improved, or rather that they were changed; and that in individual action there were moments of a peculiar quality that expressed the state in which he knew the whole earth could live all the time, and settle the hash of time, progress, and morality once and for ever. What he wanted to happen was for some man to say a word of power which should evoke this state, everywhere, not by any process, but in the twinkling of an eye. This is magic. Lovers did it, especially his lovers; and saints, when he and one or two men he knew were being saints, with a woman or so about to encourage them, at night, in a smoky room. There were moments, too, under the hills, breaking-in horses, when it came, the moment of pure being, the co-ordination of power.

But the universal word did not come off. He was over forty now, and he was losing his nerve. He was beginning to spit and sneer; and, since he could not find his word, he was beginning to grin, and hope for the world to ruin itself; and rub his hands, and tell his friends in their moments of pleasure that they were damned, not exactly because they had not listened to him, but for something rather like it. And, as very often they had listened to him, in reason, they were hurt.

Because he had not mastered the earth, he was beginning to hate it. Hate takes the grace out of a spiritual man, even his grace of body. As he left the hotel and walked west through the park, and saw the trees coming, he drew in one of his animal breaths that showed the canines under his moustache, bright like a dog. *Grin like a dog, and run about the city*; but then he understood that this was one of his empty days, which might be filled with anything or nothing.

'I must fill it,' he said, and he meant that on this day he must have a revelation and a blessing; which is a difficult thing to get to order. He went on to the grass, in among the trees, which are a proper setting for almost every kind of beauty. Their green displayed his tan and harmonized his dress. Their trunks drew attention to his height, the grass gave distinction to his walk. It was early, and there were no pretty women about to make his eyes turn this way and that, greedily, with vanity, with appeal for pity, but too scornfully for success. The trees went on growing. He looked at them and remembered Daphne, and that she had said once: 'Stop fussing, Dick. Why can't you let things alone for a bit? Think of trees.' 'Silly fool of a girl. Wanted me to make love to her, I suppose.' He had said that at the time, and he still said it, but he added Daphne to the list of people he was to see that day. Like men of his kind, at cross-purposes with their purpose, there could be nothing fortuitous that happened to him. Everything was a leading, a signature of the reality whose martyr he was; for he could never allow that he had made a fool of himself, and only occasionally that reality had made a fool of him. So he pinned the universe down to a revelation from Daphne, and took a bus to Holborn to get on with the business of the day.

It is much easier for a man to lose his self-consciousness in Holborn than in the female world of South Kensington. He went first to see a friend who was teaching a kind of Christian anarchism made dramatic by the use of Catholic ritual. He was a good man, patient with Dick, who trusted him. It was one of the things that made Dick uneasy that the works of sanctity and illumination are now distributed through offices, and he saw himself a terror to such places. His friend Eden was out. The typist was a very childish one, with short hair and a chintz overall, and she did not suggest the Sophia, the Redeemed Virgin, Dick was looking for. He shifted his expectation and saw her as the unredeemed and improbable virgin, which is the same thing as the soul of the world, and prepared to treat her for the part. He was hungry by now.

'I'm Dick Tressider,' he said, 'and I'll wait for Mr Eden.' He dropped his stick, picked it up, lit a cigarette, and walked once or twice up and down the room. 'D'you know about me?'

'I can't say that I do,' she said. 'So many gentlemen come here for Mr Eden.'

'D'you know Mr Eden well? Are you conscious of what he is doing here? I mean that it's an expression of what is happening everywhere, of what is bound to happen everywhere, man's consciousness becoming part of the cosmic consciousness?'

'Mr Eden never says anything about it.'

'D'you know this whole damned earth is going to smash any moment?'

'Mr Eden says that if there are any more wars we shall starve. He's trying to stop it.'

He grinned, and showed his wolf's teeth.

'I tell you. It'll make precious little difference what he does. You look as if you might understand. Come out and have some lunch.'

She got up obediently. She remembered that she had heard of Dick, that he had been a soldier of some family and some service. Also he was a tall figure of a man, not like the pale, ecstatic townsmen who came there.

He took her to a restaurant and ordered red wine and steak. He crammed his food down and asked her what she thought about love. Immediately she was frightened. She was not frightened of seduction or of a scene. It was pure fear. He saw that it would not do, and sulked at her, pouring down his wine.

'I don't want to waste time. I've got to get down to reality. Tell Eden I'll call in later.'

He took her out, and left her at the door of the restaurant, without a word.

He walked about London, through the streets round the British Museum, on a cool still afternoon without rain, past the interesting shops and the students, and the great building of stone. He wanted to persuade men that they were only there to illustrate the worth of the land. He did not want to see Eden, who would be busy trying to stop the next war, and getting people to dress up. He knew what war was and how it would stop these games, more power to it. It was all up with the world, and the world didn't know it. He would go to tea with Daphne now. It would be too early, but that didn't matter.

At the Museum gates he saw a man he had known who said: 'Is that you, Tressider? I didn't know you were in town.'

'I came up last night.'

'Wishing you were back?'

'Wishing I could smash these lumps of stone or get men to see their cosmic significance.'

The civilized man winced. The idea might be tolerable, but one should not say it like that.

'I am going into the Museum. Come along.'

'What are you going to do?'

'Look at things.'

'Some earth-shaking new cooking-pot?'

'It's not a question of size, is it? Come along.'

He had to run beside Dick, who flung himself over the court-yard and up the steps.

'I read a jolly fairy-story about this place,' he said. 'Some children got a magic amulet and wished the things home, and they all flew out. Those stone bull things, and all the crocks and necklaces.'

'I remember. They found a queen from Babylon, and she said they belonged to her, and wished them all home, and home they went.'

Dick looked at him with a sideways, ugly stare.

'I know. You like me, don't you, when you think I'm a fairy-boy. A kind of grown-up Puck? You like me to like rot.'

'But I do,' said his friend. 'I like that story myself, and was glad when you recalled it.'

'Do you know that the only thing we've said that meant anything was a bit of your talk – "She said they all belonged to her." That's the cursed property-sense that keeps this world a hell.'

'Oh damn the property-sense! I was going to look at the casts from Yucatan, and I always forget the way.'

Dick was staring at a case of bronze weapons. He put his hand easily on the man's shoulder. 'Don't you understand that that fairy-story is true? They could all fly away out of here. It's as easy as changing your collar.'

'Do it for us then, Tressider. I'll come along and applaud.'

'My God! You people will find a man who can do it for you, and worse things, and soon. Someone you've treated as you treat all people. Take it from me, Brooks.'

Madder than ever, thought Brooks. Won't think, and can't play. 'All right. The room is at the end. Come along.'

It is not easy to get on terms with a cast the size of a house, whose close decorations mean nothing to anyone except to an archæologist or an artist. Dick lounged and stared, and leant up against the central plaster lump.

'What are all these things for? I suppose you think you've done something when you've dug 'em up out of the earth.'

It is exceedingly difficult to explain why a thing is useful when you like it.

Dick smote it with his hand.

'A lot of good those'll do you when the world busts up.'

But Brooks was thinking what a type was there, leaning on a sacred Mayan monster, a fair, ruling, fighting, riding man, and what a twist of breeding had turned him prophet *à la* Semite, 'sad when he held the harp.' And that the harp that once – etc. – was now completely cracked.

'All right,' he said, 'we'll leave antiquities for the moment. But it's a speculation worth following: Where did that civilization come from, and did it have any contact with Egypt?'

'Egypt? They knew about the soul there, and I don't care where their jim-jam decorations came from. Civilization's going. The world wants a man whose contact is primeval.'

'Oh does it?' said Brooks. 'I suppose you mean yourself. You're about as primeval as a card-index. Come and have some tea.'

And at tea Dick asked him sweetly about his children, and sent messages to his wife, and told the story of his uncle's funeral with point and wit, and left Brooks, to go up to Daphne, with his affection intact, and his doubts.

Now it was evening. The bus climbed up the side of London, and above the screaming children and the crowd going home from work, it rolled like an animal ship; and from every contact Dick sighed and withdrew himself, until at the five roads at Camden Town he felt something coming to him which had come before. 'This place is not here,' he said. 'I can lift myself out of it, in my body. So!' He sank down a little as he said it, and answered himself. 'The things you hate are only your body being knocked about by phenomena.' Then the place disappeared, especially a public-house with a plaster tower; but there had crept up through it tall perpendicular folds, which looked like dark grey rubber, which rose and passed in from all sides. But he was free, both of the houses and of what had replaced them. He lifted himself like a clean man out of the sea, and rested in his mind, which was now full of order and peace. He wondered that he had ever minded anything, and at the end of the ride stood several men drinks in a public-house and roared with laughter with them.

Before dinner he came to Daphne's house and rang the bell. There was some time before anyone answered it. Then her old nurse came, and looked at him without knowing who he was. He came in, and took off his raincoat before he said: 'Is Miss Daphne in?'

'I'll see, sir,' she said, and led him into the living-room, which had tall windows and a balcony on to a garden full of trees. The wind, a new thing, was moving in them. It was almost night. Next door was Daphne's room. He heard the door open and shut several times, and brief voices. The room was very empty. He stumbled over a rug, and saw the shining boards and a gramophone gaping with the lid up, and records on the divan among the cushions. He did not make himself at ease by the fire. He understood that they had been dancing. He walked up and down the room, wondering what they would give him to eat.

It was all right. The peace was there. He would tell Daphne about it. Daphne would give it back to him with assent and vivid words. Perhaps he would take Daphne out to dinner. Her youngest sister came in.

'Please forgive us. We're in such a hurry. We've been dressing Daphne. Would you mind coming to see her in her room?'

He remembered Daphne's room, rows of books and glass balls and Chinese pictures of birds and windows that stepped out into the air. He followed her sister, and as he came in, heard Daphne's cry, 'Hullo, Dick!' that was like a battle yell. In a minute he was treading into a sea of tissue paper that rustled like snakes. The shutters were closed. All the lights were on. Here was night, suddenly and strongly lit. As Daphne came to meet him, her sister fell on her knees, and followed her over the carpet, pinning something at her hips.

A woman he did not know was sitting on the couch looking at Daphne. The old nurse was somewhere behind him, by the door.

'Shall I ring for a taxi, dearie?'

'In a minute, nurse, I've a few moments to spare.' Then he

trod on the paper like a man and saw her. She had on a green and white dress, and crystal earrings that touched her shoulders, and a crystal at her waist, slung round her neck with a green cord. Dick remembered enough to know that it was a dress that is not seen in shops, but is shown, *like an ear of corn reaped in silence* to certain women on certain occasions. He saw her feet in silver sandals, her hair like a black, painted doll's, a curve drawn out over each cheek. On the dressing-table, white with powder, there was a bouquet in a frill.

'Dick, I'm going out to have a glorious time.' She did not look at him twice to see what his heavy eyes said.

'Val, my dear, is my back even?' Valentine got up and took a powder-puff and dusted her sister's white back. She sat down again at her mirror, and called at him into the glass where she could see him. 'Dick, sit down. You know my cousin, Mrs Lee?' He would not know her, but sat down and stared, and saw that Daphne was like a tree in glory. And that the colour of her mouth was due to art. It was not trying to be anything else. If it was kissed, it would come off so much sticky paint. The room was warm, full of scent and whirling with powder-dust. He tried to hear the wind rising. He wanted to swear at Daphne and hit her. In the mirror, he saw her little head sink an instant. He knew her. She was thinking, 'Oh, Dick, don't spoil my pleasure.' Well, he would. Then she whipped round and smiled at him, deliberately, brutally, and he knew that he could not.

She was pulling on gloves like curd, picked up her flowers, and moved across the room.

'Nurse, ring for a taxi. Angry, Dick? I'm going to dance all night. Oh, it's good to get into decent clothes –'

He said vulgarly: 'It seems to me that you've got out of them,' and she looked at him exactly as she would look at a man of his kind who said a thing like that.

He felt his power drain out of him, his poise, assurance, pride. He had come to tell Daphne about heavenly things.

As he waited and hated her, she forgot even who he was.

'Say you like my dress. I must hear everyone say it.'

'I suppose it's fashionable, but I remember you in the shrubberies at Pharrs in a cotton dress. You came for a walk with me.'

'Oh yes. I remember Pharrs – that reminds me –'

It had not reminded her of him. She turned and went quickly to the glass again, and spoke to her cousin beside him.

'Terry. I'm not certain, but I think it wants a headdress.' She pulled out a wreath of bright green leaves and set it on her head.

They were like the leaves of no earthly laurel. He shuddered and called 'Daphne!' Her cousin agreed with her.

Her taxi came. She said: 'Dick, I'm sorry I've had no time tonight. Can I give you a lift down town?'

She flung on a silver cloak, and he followed her down the steps into the cab. The wind was rising, and drummed on the window-glass. They ran in silence down London. It was very cold. He saw where she was going; into a high square house, and down to dinner with a black and white man, down golden stairs.

She looked at him again.

'Cheer up, Dick. Don't you like to get back to it all when you come to town?'

She had won. He had not known how to express his disgust; now he did not know if he felt it.

'I suppose I miss it sometimes.'

'Look here. We've a party at the Savoy on Saturday, and we want another man. Will you come?'

He would not come. Anything might happen in the world, but he would not come.

'I'm afraid I should be out of place. You would find my change of values too complete.'

'Should we indeed! There are several Paradises, Dick. Me for this Paradise.'

She had known all the time. He must say something destructive, inimical, quickly. Only she had forgotten him again.

'Oh,' she said, 'it's cold,' and drew her silver stuff round her. Without concern he put his oily rough raincoat over the silver, the white and green, the milky back that came off a little. She made a little face, said 'Thank you' and forgot.

The wind roared through the square. She opened the door, two half-crowns in her hand.

'Here's my share. Good night, Dick. Come and see me some time. Good night, Dick.'

He did not want the taxi any more. He only wanted to meet the wind, and let Nature knock the nonsense out of him and the memories. He took the half-crowns from her, and she was out into the street before he could find his stick. He did not help her. She was gone. The wind roared past. He paid the man, and at the last instant before night, saw her run up the steps, and the wind take her cloak and open it. He saw her bend like a full sail, and balance to the wind. He saw her head go down, and her silver shoes run up. The door opened; he saw her run into a tall yellow arch, and the black door immediately close on her again.

From Altar to Chimney-Piece

He was exquisitely in love with Paris, his *sweet profound Paris*.
Great Paris –
    where the sights are –
    and the nights are
    and the lights are.

In love as young Englishmen used to fall in love with her, who had come to her just after the War, after doctors and hospitals and sanatoria had done their best and their worst for them. After the country-life prescribed had done its best; and after a year or more had sent them out with the minute drop of sap, without which health of body is no more than the carrying-round of an active corpse and health of spirit does not exist, running once more in their blood. A supreme tonic was all that was needed, and here Paris played its lovely part; and, though it seems incredible now, just that part of Paris the newspapers have learned to leer at, which has now become an American side-show and an alcoholics' parade, Montparnasse. Montparnasse – at that time still old and shabby and merry and wearing a crown of little stars at night. Twelve years ago, when Vincent first went there, it was still like that, still French, still serenely uncomfortable, still adorable and full of great and famous people and those who would become great. Famous Americans too, but come to enjoy France, not a bad copy of New York. Their imitators, their failures, their complex-ridden repression-loosers had not yet arrived to violate and corrupt it. It was not until five years ago or six, that a demon of vile intelligence stepped off the boat-train, crossed the Seine at the Pont Royal, followed up the Boulevard Raspail to where it meets the Boulevard Montparnasse, and at that wide, untidy, sun-struck, tram-clanging cross-roads halted to see what he could do to change all that. He found a quarter in a princess of cities where people were being good because they were being happy, because, after the lost years, a small tide of earthly joy was rising gently in that place. Or winding in and out of it like a little stream no evil thing could cross. A place where, even if people suffered, the sorrow had in it something that was exquisite, a touch of rapture, as though the pain was about something real, a necessary part of something like immortal life. A place where men and women were beginning to live again, beginning to make up for the years that the War had taken. A place where work was being done, by people of all kinds and races; and France at her work again, modulating, civilizing, evoking, praising, setting free.

In those days you could see, springing, timid but sturdy, like plants an east wind has shrivelled to the earth, but whose roots have lived, men and women in bud again, hardly able to believe the blue air's caress, on the warm soil firm and nourishing, but lulled by them and fed – looking out at life again from the shoulders of Paris, from the arms of France.

This story, suppose one could bear to write it, is not about how the demon changed all this, how those who should have guarded the stream let him across. Or how, like a good strategist, he attacked the French where they are weakest, telling the proprietors of hotel or restaurant or café how much money they could make by giving the nastier or more ignorant kind of American the drains and baths and bars he thinks are civilization, because they are all he has to distinguish him from the least finished kind of man. Hell found no difficulty in transporting them, the men and women who think art synonymous with vice, and delirium tremens an ornament if acquired in an artists' quarter. These and the hangers-on of all the arts, their failures, the silly-rich, the neurotic, the intolerably-repressed. They came – and the place is hardly recognizable now. They came – demoralizing their hosts, who grew fat and brutal and time-serving under the rush of dollar bills. They came – and the old delights went, the love of work and the love of play. The love of a party, work, solitude, study, indolence or an exhilarating row. Love of loving Paris, of good wine, good food; love of one's friends, one's enemies, one's beloved. The lovers went, as the old cafés were pulled down or came back after an interval of hammers and scaffolding in new and horrible clothes, with doubled prices and waiters ravenous for tips, and with no eye for the old clients who made or would make their Quarter and their service illustrious. The great arts withdrew with the men and women who practised them, and with them went the lovers and the men and women who were beginning to live again. They went – to be replaced by the parasites on all the arts and all the passions, the men and women harlots and the fashionable purveyors of sexual excitements disguised as art. And with these, *their* panders, not of social or sexual tastes, but the neurotic vices which follow fashion and have nothing to do with desire. Also the men and women whose hell had not been occasioned by any dislocation of our society, but by the putrid state of their subconscious selves, occasioned by fear, by over-indulgence, and sometimes by the intolerable repression of American life.

Anyhow, their arrival closed Montparnasse as a temple of Æsculapius; and Vincent, the young man who began this story, went to live in another quarter; and for a time, again, it was well with him.

Years passed, and Paris remained in part his home; and as happens to people who become imaginatively conscious of a great city, he came to have a private map of it in his head. A map in which streets and groups of buildings and even the houses of friends were not finally relevant, or only for pointers towards another thing, the atmosphere or *quality* of certain spots or spaces or groups. These maps are individual to each lover of a city, charts of his translation of its final significance, of the secret workings of men's spirits, which, through the centuries, have saturated certain quarters, giving them not only character and physical exterior, but quality, like a thing breathed. Paris is propitious for this making of magic maps. While one thing that Vincent, the Cornish gentleman, found out was that the hillside, across the river from the Tour St Jacques to the top of the Rue du Cardinal Lemoine is still given over to witchcraft, a winding stream of passionate and infernal air, in and out of the old Latin Quarter. Also that, in Passy, there is a river-strip and a small low terrace (now in the hands of housebreakers), looking across to the river over green tree-tops where the tears cried in the Revolution are still audible. A blind rain among the almost visible gleam of ancient silks, the tapping of heels, the stir of powder, a terrace where the soul of elegance still breathes, and, like a heart beating, one hears the passionate continuity of French life.

In the Rue St Dominique it is difficult to tell the living from the dead, and he could never be sure if he were not buying cherries off a talking ghost. The west wind sweeps them out like leaves, in handfuls, especially at dusk, when the Eiffel Tower is putting on its crown and the necklace which hangs to its feet; while the wind roars in the mouths of old courtyards, springs like a cat in and out of their corners, and with its broom sends out spinning leaves, torn papers, ghosts and the street-swarm, to scatter them on the starry, roaring space before the Invalides; where, looking down towards the river, you can see Imperial Paris with its crowns and tower. For Paris is a city divided – not like London, with all that she has of splendour and government, of learning or pleasure or art on one bank of its stream; and the other a place not one half of the city has ever set foot in, being given over to workmen at their meanest. But of Paris it can be said that the right bank of the Seine belongs to the world, and the left bank to France. This could have been said once, and is still partly true – but this story is not about a city, a few bars only out of the Song of Paris, and perhaps, of something more than Paris. So that for its introduction, a few notes on the present state of that capital will serve.

Two years after the War imagine Vincent at least half-healed, and as the years pass, see him half-established there, but going less and less often to his first love, the quarter of Montparnasse. He has struck roots here and there, in a small Passy flat and in several French homes, in a few cafés and restaurants and among certain groups, English and American. He would arrive now at any time or leave – for his small, ancient home and estate, which was in Cornwall, and of which he was a careful steward. Less consciously now and more by habit he would leave England – for that exhilaration which is also rest, for that delight which is peace and Paris's loveliest secret. For, like many men of profound patriotism, he liked less and less the way England was going, what she was doing, and still less what was being done to her.

While this also was true and he knew it, that, since the War, he had never achieved full life again, not quite. He did his duty as a small country gentleman, kept up his classics, his science, his contemporary letters, his friends. Had neither – and he noticed the omission – either love-affairs or any work that implied creation. Not up to the limit of his powers. For he was a man to whom quiet power would have come in life, in his case perhaps in moderate public life, with a fair chance, too, of private and enduring passion. 'They castrated me, after all,' he used to tell himself. 'I'm just wholly alive, but only just. I can't use all of myself. Like a man who plays clock-golf perfectly, but not on the links. There must be a million or so like me.' Not quite forty, he had not given up the hope that the check was inside himself, that the minute barring of his energies and impulses would disappear of itself, if the right, exactly the right, stimulus came. Scrupulously honest, he was hard with himself: gave life every chance to have its way with him. And it seemed that life delicately evaded him. 'It is like being thirsty, a thirst only one drink would satisfy, and I don't know its name. Still less if it'll ever be offered. Neither I nor anyone who is in the same boat.' This is not a state which can be talked about, but Vincent was a much-liked man. A man, lacking at any time the power to seize life by the throat and strangle it into submission, he was one of those who work joyfully for whatever in their age is best. The stuff out of which the 'perfect, gentle knight' was made; and at any time, in war or medicine, in government or agriculture, in works of organization or mercy – a man who needed, for his full development, a law, a worship, if possible a congregation, and a church. At best, a hero. These he was equally without, in the west of England from where he came by long descent, or in France. Or among his friends, who were all in the same state; who also, that being one of the reasons why they were his friends, knew it. The adventures of such men are important because, whether they are fatal or not, they are honourable adventures, and because they are significant of our time. For it seems that none of their traditional occupations are able to take them over and use them as they once did, neither religion nor politics nor any traditional occupation, no cause or leader or conception of human relations with the divine. However they have survived as individual souls, the same minute sap-gland, in them just saved, seems to have dried up in the clan and the group – almost in the nation; and its loss has left the most vital of human affairs somehow inadequate. Insufficient to take a man by the shoulders and swing him off into full allegiance, able at once to take the rough with the smooth, to judge as well as to save; to pour a life into a chosen mould, and feel it in the end sufficient, a mirror for all that there is. What is wrong? Was it his own fault? It was too easy to say 'yes' to that. While he knew that he was not without ambition, and that it has never been easier than it is today for a man to boil his own egg. And not only the worst men. There is still a modest place for the Vincents. Only Vincent who had never wanted more than a modest place, whose instinct was to give his life up to something greater than himself, found that he did not want *that* modest place.... He had a dream of himself as a little fish, standing on its tail and bowing to one of the present Great – say a newspaper Lord – on an Albert Memorial throne and being asked why he did not do anything. His answer was like the Bible: 'Because no man has hired me.' On which the man on the throne would begin to tell him all the things which a 'straight, intelligent Englishman of goodwill' ought to be doing. He heard himself say 'I'd sooner be a dago-moron than serve you: but I'm a fish: that lets me out.' And then he tried to run away on the point of his tail, until he noticed he had changed into the little Sea Maid who walked on knives. But that was for love's sake. For what love was he bearing a life-time's loss of honourable employment? For a love which had left the earth? Gone off somewhere behind a space-time curtain into the inconceivable?

It was this that drew him and his friends to artists. They had something. Mysteriously, tiresomely, or noisily or crossly, or savagely or piteously, the arts went on, weathering the chill dark storm, blowing across the earth as if from outer space. Yes, art was still going on, most certainly in literature and particularly in Paris. The men and women who did it had something they held to and which held them. Theirs was essential health, and it was among their hangers-on, or – and here he smiled – among their admirers, that the death-rate was so high. But all men cannot be working artists, not in the strict sense. If the artists' secret was one form of a universal secret, there must be a re-statement of it, in terms equally life-giving, for his sort of man, for every sort of man. Nor was it, he suspected, quite enough even to meet the artists' full needs. For two things are needed today, an art in the terms of Dante or Æschylus, which is also first-class in terms of our age and of itself.

When he came to think of it, he did not know any writer or any painter whose work fulfilled such terms; but only for such would their art be enough. While they were all suffering from a singular new set of prohibitions: forbidden in the past to refer to the Deity as a wish-fulfilment, they now seemed unable to refer to It as anything else: unable to mention the lavatory, they forced the reader to spend more time there than he would in fact. While the bed, once tabu because too stimulating, now appeared discouragingly as a trap, baited with all the ills that flesh is heir to, source of disease and abortion; or, if not in the body, of the cruellest terrors of the minds. As for painting! Why was Titian able to paint a picture of Sacred and Profane Love, while, today, no one but a bad painter would try? Vincent noticed all this, noticed also that, traps or not, beds did not come into his life, who filled them with no more than his own lean body that he kept in scrupulous condition – for what?

Time after time, a moment would come and a desire – to fling himself out, abandon himself to the flashing hurry of contemporary affairs as they tore past him, a ravelled web of cross-colours, a stream whose rapids so many bodies he knew were shooting, their heads bobbing under and out, their hair splashed with spray. Or piled like mounting salmon before some obstacle. Which usually turned out not to be there. Or, more frequently, turned out not to be the barrier they thought, but something different, neither to be changed nor circumvented. Part of the structure of reality, in fact.

Still, he envied these swimmers, those delicate or vigorous, fastidious or powerful specialists in pleasure or dissipation, in the pursuit of power or wealth or notoriety, or of social or sexual success – rioting in their Paris-playground, incomparable *terrain* where, for once *'work was play and play was life'*. But what play? And what life? He sneered, as near as ever he came to a sneer, at it and at his inability to yield to it. While the image of the Poor Fish pursued him and distressed him.

Par délicatesse
j'ai perdu ma vie.

Here his humility protested. Who was he to compare himself
with Rimbaud? If he had chosen to forget 'the ardours of an
incomparable adolescence', it was because he had preferred to
go about his own mysterious and delectable business. Vincent's
youth had passed on Vimy Ridge, in hospital, and on the Somme.

Meanwhile, there were the artists of contemporary Paris, and
the modest collection, part prudent investment, he was making
to set on the shelves and along the panels of a Cornish manor-
house. There an Atlantic sun and airs from half-way across a
planet would look in on the café scenes, the abstract plates, plants,
pots, and musical instruments, the austere landscape, the magic
horses of contemporary painting.

'I have brought back tangible treasure,' he would console himself – 'for the more I look at some of these, the more I like them.
I have brought back, too, a piece of France.' Noticing that whoever
brings home French work, does that; and finally, that what he
had acquired, owed as much to the spirit of the land as to any
particular painter. Or, in another way, that in France, the most
individual artists are more the transmitters of a supreme tradition
than of themselves. Matchless discipline! Was he dying slowly
for want of the version of it proper to himself?

If he had been driven away from the famous cross-roads where
his life in Paris had begun, there was still a half-way house; still
in the Latin Quarter, still itself, still brimming with young life; a
place where there remained a taste of the old delights – the Café
des Deux Magots on the Boulevard St Germain. At the end of
the still noble part of a noble street, on the edge of the space in
his map coloured 'witchcraft', it stands close to the river at its
most adorable strip – the Quai Voltaire. He would sit there, with
the pleasure at the back of his mind that comes from the right
geographic situation, from being perfectly placed with regard to
the whole environment. At any moment he could get up and go
for an enchanting walk, with, a few yards off as he crossed his
sorcerer's line, a hint of danger about it. A delicious sense of
walking into the part of a town which was literally supernatural,
charged with it, a charge put in during a part of the Middle Ages,
too strong to wear off. Also that he, and a good proportion of its

inhabitants, were in tacit agreement about it – and the less said the better. Meanwhile, one could always retreat, back to 'the Maggots', as a swimmer out of the haunted caves of ocean to the warm beaches of a pleasant shore.

It was there that he met his American girl.

She was that freest of free things – a young woman sent with her people's blessing and a sufficient allowance to stay in Europe as long as she liked. (He could never quite make out what her people were, her credentials were not those of some of the New Englanders he knew; but he judged the situation to be that.) Of course she was to return – to an address which geographically baffled him – filled with the last culture; her pretty gift for painting improved, with ravishing clothes and interesting friends. Something like that seemed to be the old peoples' kindly wish, not nervous about her – that, heaven bless it! not in their tradition – for she had friends who would keep an eye on her, and her own good sense would keep off undesirable foreigners. There would be plenty of the right American boys there, for sure.

This, at any rate, was Vincent's kindly translation. He saw her saffron scarf fluttering along the Boulevard one spring morning, heard her little heels tapping on the pavement and 'registered' – the word had just come in – nothing but delight. She *was* enjoying herself, bless her! He saw her eating cream-topped ices and wave her spoon; and when some friends of his spoke to her, he spoke to them; and finally took her to a place where the ices were larger and better, and fed her several more. So they became friends.

After that he saw her every day, with that utter Paris-freedom which allows people to do exactly what they want to do. Not all people. In practice, the people who achieve it are the people who are 'most right'. Others, unless they are strong in character or long practised in evil-doing, find that liberty a snare at least; at most, a terrible thing. These fall continually into traps they have set for themselves, create imaginary barriers and fall down before them, feel emptiness where others find open air, and conjure up demons to people it. She was not like that, he said, his lass with the delicate bones, her coaxing, slightly hoarse voice, her sharp young appetite for everything. Vincent immediately forgot to think of himself as a piece of middle-aged war breakage, and tore round with her all night and half the day.

If he had thought of himself as a little older or a little younger, it would have been better. Older, he would have assumed authority; younger, he would not have thought to let her be. As it was, he used often to withdraw himself respectfully, in a sort of homage to her youth. While all the time he noticed that he was asking himself questions about her. For one thing, he could not find out how much she really knew. Was she really so keen on everything, and so intelligently? Or was she – it was an uncomfortable suspicion – a kind of wonderfully trained automaton, for response to whatever was presented to her, but without criticism and without real choice? Without effective memory, and the working-over the creation it implies. *Was* it sheer youth, trying everything at once? (Or was it looking for and would it find something that was outside the range of his understanding at all?) Was she a puppet, who might even now be dancing to lures he had never heard? Or a bit of both? The last presented appalling difficulties. Suppose the part of her that was not an exquisite doll had no connection or the slightest real interest in what was important to Vincent, to Vincent's race, to high European life? Suppose she represented another, an in-the-bone-and-nerve raw thing, a tricky race- mixing? A wild animal with an instinct for adaptability, inquiring- ness and protective mimicry that masked – well, something that since the Stone Ages man has been muzzling, keeping on a lead, destroying, lest it should destroy him – even though it were one of his eyes, a part of his right hand? He could not place her in any of the Americas he knew something of, in New England or the South or the East or well-accounted for New York. While 'from somewhere near Kansas City' – and where *is* Kansas City? – was the nearest he ever understood of her address.

These tiresome questions represent the further side of the moon of his love for her, the questions, as he afterwards remembered, he had put about her from the first; that had grown until they made shrill noises at him, in proportion to his love, the other, the visible side of the moon. Was she real, or was she not? For if she were real, his real, she was too good to be true. If the child were true, there was no imagining how far she would go, nor the miracle it would be to have the care of her, 'to watch, to encourage, to restrain, the royal young creature by his side'. Was she infinitely sophisticated? Or nobly innocent? Or of such intelligence and native virtue that she *did* know, dealing with good and evil like a young warrior from heaven? Her 'Come on, Vincent', 'Look Vincent' – her eyes, the curve of her parted lips – was their strength that of a spirit or a wild beast?

It was one of Vincent's simplicities that he did not see what value he might have had for her; or that, whatever she was, she was a young girl, and so, to some extent, what the man who took her in hand expected her to be. That what he had to do was to assert himself, muffle any protests with 'that's what matters over here, sweetheart' and a kiss. He had not learned from life how much time and trouble kisses save, still less the romantic figure he might have seemed to her, had he been a little more explicit, had not assumed that she could place him as an English girl would have placed him; not realizing that where the tradition is different, a common language may be a trap. In fact he made most of the mistakes that we make in dealing with young America.

What happened, when it happened, happened quickly. The quickening appalled him, who forgot that however long it may take to prepare, a fall is a matter of seconds. Later he reminded himself, that if it had not happened, he would have given himself up to his love. Taken back with him to the West Country a strange woman; and that it was not without some mercy – even her mercy – that he had been prevented. That if he had seen an infernal curtain lifted, he had been left with a closer apprehension of the world. For a curtain was lifted for him, but not before the last minute of the last act. The rest of the story had been played on the stage of Paris, as if before one of those drop-scenes which came down close to the footlights, leaving the stage a strip, for the actors to enter in twos and threes and the chorus to dance across. A drop only lowered for scenes whose significance is momentary, while the full stage is being set behind.

They went about with artists as before, but Vincent's friends were usually English or some French; it was Cherry, the girl, who had discovered and furiously cultivated some of the Americans; who, so far as he could see, had taken over all that was left of Montparnasse. He found himself telling her: 'Of course you have to make an art of your own now. Your great men of letters were so much part Europe gone across the Atlantic. Now you've half a continent wanting to express itself, instead of just New

England. Though how the place managed to breed Melville and Poe...' But these, as he expected, she had hardly read, while the others were no more than school-books to her. What excited her was a number of quite young men and women, whose master was James Joyce; and what *they* were about, he could never quite determine. Unless it was to turn themselves inside out. Very natural to youth, but he did not much like their interiors, not quite whole-somely raw they seemed, and furtive and afraid, wanting in candour and simplicity of perception, in faith and essential courage or the rudiments of fine taste. He even called them to himself a set of unprincipled little bastards, blackguards or milksops in the mak-ing. Which was not at all fair; but, in his heart, he was blaming them for having hurt his Paris, who of all their countrymen were least responsible; whom poverty kept reasonably sober, who were not to be blamed for not knowing what they really wanted, or for the growing-pains of a nation, or for homes where the wrong things were held in esteem. For in America it would seem that a cheap and strident idealism often takes the place of true discip-line, the love of country or of mankind. All this he made himself allow for, reduced himself to wishing and wondering why, with all their chances, these boys made no effort to make over their lives with some sobriety, pray for peace and quiet and practise them. They spoke as though nothing had ever happened before they happened. What was worse, they wrote – some of them – as though man had never put pen to paper before. Incidentally he noticed that they were not without friends among certain young Frenchmen, busy on the same experiments. But, then, on this last point, the Frenchmen would not be able to judge.

Perhaps the abyss that Vincent saw opened, that for an instant he leaned over, gave him a glimpse of something final, as the colour of the infernal spectrum might be held, for a split second, in a drop of dew. While if, at the same time, his glimpse was his salvation, the danger and the escape came together oddly mixed, treading on each other's heels. And it was with difficulty that his mind held, clearly and continuously, what he had seen. As he told it to himself and as I learned it from him, he called it 'the translation of a translation of a translation'.

'We're at least two languages out,' he said. 'But at least we both make the same thing of it.'

What happened was this.

Between Montparnasse and the Boulevard St Germain, the tide-line between the rest of the city and his magical strip, there lived an old woman of some consequence, in herself like a received and accepted and perfectly reputable witch. A local sorceress, and therefore, to some extent, international, long become part of the landscape – who *might* accept an invitation to a fashionable christening, but had never been known to resent it if she were not asked. Her spells were composed with the help of the English language used as if it had never been used before; and were not calculated to inspire fear. She had a house in impeccable taste. Her entertainments were formal and much sought after. But the people who were always to be found there were Cherry's young Americans. And their French friends. The art of the latter was based, partly on a mystical reliance on the subconscious, partly on extreme Communist theory. In essence a belief in magic – '*Le Moi est le Verbe, et le Verbe c'est Dieu*'. In practice, a measured brutality, a logic of destruction, all somehow made elegant, flashed with 'chic' by the qualities of the French mind, its instinct for proportion – even in the realm of chaos and old night. While for reasons Vincent could not make out, the French who knew everything and the Americans who knew nothing, met, at the house of the old woman in a kind of uneasy dance.

One day it was Cherry who insisted that he should visit her. He asked: 'Why do you young things go there? Why do you want to go? You can't have much fun. Your best behaviour and no drinks. Yet I believe you spend half your time there, when you aren't with me. While what I'd like to know is – which is the agreeable change from which?'

She gave him a little smile with closed lips, what he thought of after as a far-too-wise smile.

'She's an old dame of course. I reckon she likes it that way.'

'Why should a flibberty-gibbet like you mind what she likes?' The girl hadn't an answer – she evaded all such answers. Yet go she would, and now she would have him go with her; and amused Vincent by telling him how very carefully he must behave. Though he did not believe it was snobbery; always he had felt her to be far more interested in her boyfriends than in any of his celebrities. He did not know what to make of it. He flung it away from him, determined to make nothing of it at all.

From the beginning he had loved her. For the last few days he had fallen in love with her. No one knows what that is – only the infinite variations of what it looks like. But this one property it always has, that the beloved becomes harmonized in the lover's sight. As though seen in some magical glass, which mankind has always insisted, and probably rightly, that the image it gives is nearer to reality than any other. Closer for the instant, but liable to vanish, liable also to burden the original with its loveliness – (for it is rare, for women, at least, to wish to live up to the image the lover has seen). So Vincent saw Cherry now, marvellously the same, but now all true, all one. Girl of the Golden West, young maid *'prochaine Aphrodite'*, ready for adventure, yet a wife in the making. He would take her back to the West Country for her journey's end – the end that is a beginning; incorporate her into the saga of England by way of the saga of his house. He had put it to her lightly, a few nights before, during a wild evening in Montmartre. She had danced away, said 'no', implied 'yes'. It was the look in her darkening eyes he had not understood.

He was now asking her again:

'Cherry, my heart, will you make up your mind to it and marry me?' She became very serious:

'Sure, I ought to tell you. You come up to tea with me at Miss Van Norden's, and after that you'll know – I mean, I'll know – I mean –.' So he had seen many small beasts pursued and casting around, but he was not thinking of things like that. He drew her hands to him and kissed her small brown wristbones. For the last week, a clean and quiet content had been entering his life, as a man sees – not the other side of a wood, but a path that will lead him there; and already, ahead, a thinning of dark branches, a promise of open country not too far off, at last. As, with a turn of passion, he drew her to him, she did not draw her wrists away; it felt almost as though she were pressing them against his mouth. He expected her to dance off, but instead he saw her, now standing upright, straight before him, a young gold tree between him and the Paris-winter fire. A moment later, she was fallen between his knees and her shell-curled head was burrowing blind towards him. She was saying: 'You're strange too. It's another kind of strange, but I tell myself it's the kind of sort that's quiet because it's strong, and so strong it can afford to be kind. Like one kind

of strength, whatever people say. Sort of thing I thought I wanted
– till I found out something else. Or what I'm like myself. I
thought *that'd* cure me of being afraid, but maybe it hasn't. I'm
not sure I'm not afraid still of what they call life –.' He supposed
that she meant that life hadn't turned out what she had expected,
not like *him*. That she expected him to give her courage again;
and he was filled with the infinite – there is no other word –
delight of the lover on whom the beloved calls for help.

'Life,' he said, cheerfully, 'it's our friend from now on.' He
gathered her up. It was all right. The beginning of the way: first
with this precious thing –

'I didn't know that you'd found life too much already.'

'Like hell I have!' She answered harshly, with a wriggle out of
his arms, where for a minute or more she had lain exquisitely,
and a spring on to the arm of his chair. He saw her face in the
mirror. It had not the Artemis-look of the girl he had met a year
ago – but the look of another hunter, who had become the hunted.
A song tolled in his head: –

> Thy lovers were all untrue,
> Thy chase had a beast in view,
> Thy lovers were all untrue.

Then:

> Time the old year was out –

What sort of a passing-bell was it? A rare accompaniment for a
man about to take his young love out to tea.

They left his warm flat and went down the wide, shallow French
stairs, side by side. In the grey street he thought that the small
gilt curls growing under her scarlet hat were like some delicious
fruit, gilding winter with promise; and that her face and her slight
body and flying legs made her like a boy-angel. He strode beside
her, tall with pride and possession, and approval that she should
choose to walk, like a country-girl and not like a town miss; and
that her walk was fit for the wild land, hills and dark valleys and
hollows and sea-terraces, where her home would be.

They reached the house of the old woman, across a courtyard
in which there were true city trees, whose branches stirred in the
small bleak wind as though they wept. The long room was full,

and he, except his hostess, the oldest person there. Why was it full of young men? Why should they go there? Cherry seemed to know them all. English or French. While it had about it the indefinable air of a group, meeting in a familiar place. But what a place to choose, an entertainment as conventional, indeed it reminded him of it, as the hospitality of a cathedral close. If indeed the Frenchmen found the formality agreeable, would the American boys, come to Europe, as he knew, to throw off all restraint?

There was tea on an ancient table, before a magnificent fire. Their hostess sat and spoke to them, one by one; giving the newcomer a little more of her attention. Then he noticed that, after a time, people found themselves in circulation. One after another, in twos and threes, and one or two accompanied by her, they would make the circle of the long room, down whose centre ran more heavy tables. Exceedingly slowly they went, a flowing stream, turning their heads up from left to right to look up at the celebrated collection of pictures, or down on to the tables, at books and manuscripts and *objets d'art*. With pauses and repetitions, jerks and restarts, but always round and round the same way, counter-clockwise; so that, unless you caught someone up – and that you somehow felt was a thing you should not do – you hardly met anyone who was there.

The first time, the old woman herself had taken him. He saw Cherry with a pale Frenchman, what he thought of as five bars ahead. The pictures were superb and he enjoyed them. But when he spoke to her across the tables, he felt that he had not been discreet. Much later, when he had been round again, once with a stranger, once by himself, he anchored himself with a bun and more tea in a dim corner, and it came to him how strange it was; and that this was a place where this party was going on all the time, a ritual of some particular significance, a kind of enchantment. (In situation the house was off his magic-map, too far west, between Raspail and the Boul' Miche. He remembered this almost with relief.)

It grew dark. Candles, many of them and nothing else, were lit. He still sat in his corner, his tea-cup balanced on his knee, opposite a famous picture which was his excuse.

For many years after that winter evening's entertainment, he ground and burrowed into his memory to recover how Cherry had appeared. They had hardly spoken to one another, he purposely insisting on nothing, believing that she was trying to see what he looked like among her friends. All that he could, with infinite effort, recall, was that she had been very quiet, possibly uneasy, respectful even to the old woman, who, and he disliked her for it, patronized the girl as though she had been some little silky dog. Again, that on their round-the-table dance, she had been partnered by a pale young Frenchman, in a light suit. The dying light had shown up his bright hair, the dull white skin of his nose and forehead. This was the sharpest image Vincent's memory threw upon the screen; and that he had called the Frenchman's hair 'green-gold' and smiled at it and had not liked him. His eyes were probably grey to match, and Vincent's mind insisted that they were red-flecked on the whites and red-rimmed. He had seen that, inside his slack clothes, his body was slack and would be slacker. Cherry and he had talked, when they had spoken at all, without looking at one another. Her French had remarkably improved, low and vibrating. That was all. All. All. All. Night-out, day-in, he could recall no more. The talk of the room – in rapid French or most pronounced American, ran past him. All gossip or the latest experiments in the Arts. That was the old woman's *forte*, as all Paris knew. The stratum of public-school boy which underlay so many of Vincent's judgments, kept insisting that if they were really doing so much to the Arts, they would talk about it less: until his sense of justice corrected him, reminding him that they were in France, where it is not incorrect to speak of things of the mind.

Yet everything in the room that had to do with the Arts was ancient, and the picture that had anchored him, a Fragonard. While, among so much lively and controversial youth, the decorum was peculiar. There was animation, no doubt, but spiritually, if not actually, in whispers. His own lass had appeared actually prim. It had been, too, something more than repression; there was something automatic about it, as of a coterie, a set, repeating what they had often done before; and, behind the hypnotic winding round and round the room, as though there was something known – to everyone in the room but him; something – these were the words that rose – large and raw, yet exceedingly subjective; a common knowledge, a secret, even a mysticism, funny, beastly, witty, mad, untrue – but neither mad enough nor false enough to be inoperative and inactive. Yes, there was a secret in that room. He had quickly become aware of it, but not at the time with any reference to Cherry; Cherry who was walking in his mind in a cup of wind and a lance of sunlight off the Atlantic, where England begins to thrust its bones up out of the sea.

Nor did he wonder, at the time, why she had so completely deserted him, his sensibility suggesting to him that girls at such moments are apt to hide. Nor did he give a thought to the young Frenchman, except to wonder if he had seen him, as he had certainly seen some of the American boys, enjoying themselves in a very different manner elsewhere. Certain of them, highly intoxicated: up to larks, in fact.

It was time to go. He looked round the room at the figures passing. The girl did not look up at him, he had to fetch her. They went out together silent; and when they got into the taxi they were silent. They parted to change and he took her out to dinner; and after dinner she told him that she would not marry him. As she said it, he knew she would not: he would never take her home to the West, nor would they, two lovers, play hide-and-seek there, in and out the curtains of the wind. A sea-noise rose in his head.

'You made up your mind then this afternoon, my dear?'

'Yes, I suppose so. I told you I'd tell you.'

'But you haven't told me enough: I mean what it would be fair for me to know. What was it that decided you?' (It means so much to know that: then you know who your enemy is, and believe, at the instant, that you have only to know who he is to destroy him.) Cherry was looking at him wretchedly.

'I'm not going to explain. I know all right. You take it from me – you'll be glad enough.'

'You mean, don't you, that I shall find something out? I don't care if I do. You mean that you've been having an affair with someone else, and perhaps you can't make up your mind? I'd understand that. While you're only a child, and I can be of use to you.' She began to laugh, a miserable laugh, but with a note in it that made him recoil – a movement in the mind which often alters, and for good, the previous angle of vision. It was bad, that laugh, a note in it at once curt and unpleasant, as though there was a dirty impulse behind it. Not the laughter of a slip of the moon. She was saying:

'Had an affair! Can't make up my mind! Be of use to me! Who in hell cares for you and your uses? Child am I! Bet your grand-mother – Who cares about being fair to you, you poor fish?'

'I for one,' said Vincent, a touch of anger helping him. (All the time she was on the edge of crying, which made her actual words less significant.) He went on: 'You had not made up your mind until this afternoon. I think you had better tell me, for, one way or another, I mean to find out.' It hurt him to see her slightness, trying to bury itself in the folds and the fur of her cloak.

'Go on and find out then.'

'So I shall. As a matter of fact, you're going to tell me now.'

'Why in hell should I?'

'Because I'm going to leave you with the memory that you'd that much courage.' She said hurriedly in a low voice:

'It sounds somehow different in English, but you can take it I was in with that set before ever I knew you: belonged there: wouldn't leave them if I could. You were Blaise's joke. That's why I told you you'd be glad to be out of it.'

'In with what bunch?'

'The lot there – there this afternoon. You can make what you like of it.' Then he remembered the young Frenchman. She sprang up. He saw her out of the restaurant, into a taxi; and came back to his table, the room swimming across his eyes.

Several days passed before he pulled himself together enough to do a little serious thinking. *What* was behind it all? He was not so stupid as not to know once he came to think of it that he had a great deal to offer the girl. Why had he been only a joke? Had he been *only* a joke? He asked himself the rejected lover's ques-tions: 'Where did I go wrong? Who did she prefer to me? What should I have done *"to lure this tassel-gentle to my wrist"*?' That she had perched there an instant, several instants, he knew. What had scared her off? He suffered, not, as he knew after a short time, so much for her, as for what she had meant to him. By means of her he had sensed a way by which his full life would have been restored to him. She was not that life, or only a part of it, but married to her, he would have been able, at last, to use all of himself. Nor had his love been selfish, he would have done his best to insure the same fullness, of thought and experience, for her also.

How had they missed it? What was the meaning of that laugh? He remembered her warm confidence at first, in the summer and in the spring. That had not been *all* acting. In the early autumn he had lost sight of her, but not for long. What had happened during that time? And, above all, what part had the shadowy room in the house whose doors gave on to the courtyard full of weeping trees – what part had it played, and its mistress? Conscious inquiry came hardly to him, outside his code and training, near spying; until he remembered a Frenchwoman of distinction who knew everything that happened in Paris, and went to call on her.

Alone, in her salon, she spoke very readily indeed. As a matter of fact, his simplicity took her in, and she imagined nothing personal in his curiosity; while it amused her to display the strangenesses of her city to a well-bred man from another land.

From her he learned what he instantly felt that he had known all the time – that the young Frenchmen – she could not answer for '*ces Américains*' – who went to the old woman's house were a very bad lot indeed. Of course their idea, as they explained it to the Paris public, was to make as close a copy as they could of the principles and practices of Revolutionary Russia. '*Ces sales Bolsheviks*' were their masters, which meant in practice chiefly in their sexual conduct. It was the same in their art; but there, as many of them had talent, the results were sometimes stimulating, exciting, and anyhow very much *à la mode*. But in themselves they were horrible young people. They played obscene practical jokes; they had a cult of cruelty – psychological cruelty; and those whose nerves would stand it, made a study and a practice of physical torture. They stole things, very cleverly too, for an excellent joke and a high feather in their caps; there were people in prison on their account. They had a system of blackmail which helped them to live – they were quite open about it – called it a protest against bourgeois morality. But what made it quite intolerable, what, as Vincent agreed, implied a particularly nasty mixture of ignorance

and hypocrisy, was their spirit of which they boasted of cold sci-
entific inquiry. Dragging science into that *galère*. Of course, she
added – she was a really intelligent woman – Russia was just an
excuse, or possibly, and in parts, a useful model. It had happened
before, was happening perhaps in a lesser degree everywhere,
the cult of *'le Moi'* in excelsis, and of the private dream. In Art,
a cult of the arbitrary use of words to express the private dream.
Of course, if your dreamer were a Rimbaud or a Mallarmé, you
got an art to match. 'Art,' said Vincent, 'is not life. At least...'
'Exactement,' said the Frenchwoman, and that whatever the art of
the private dream might be, the life of it was another thing; usually
a much nastier thing. 'Subjectively run mad,' said Vincent, 'but
it would all depend upon the dream.' 'And what sort of stuff are
the run of our dreams made of?' said the Frenchwoman. 'Who
out of a million has an inspired dream? While for the rest...'
'Where will it take them?' said Vincent. 'To suicide, often,' was
the answer, 'or back into the Church.' She then asked if we had
such phenomena in England. He considered. He supposed that
we had, though he had never met it; that it must happen, but less
publicly, less in groups, perhaps less staged. Tentatively, that
would do. 'I believe,' he said, 'that we're a less intelligent, certainly
about æsthetics, but a more sensible, people. We do not laugh at
life or at each other so brilliantly as you do, but we do laugh at
ourselves. I can't see one of us setting out to be a conscientious
blackmailer or a thief on principle. Though I've known seduction
carried out that way. An English boy of gifts, however bad his
character, would find it too much to believe that there was nothing
in the Universe except what he and a few of his friends felt. Even
if he knew the arguments. For there is a logic of it.

'But tell me some more about it. Have they any women among
them?'

'What young men will always have. A number of young women
who like them, and so pretend to understand and adore what
they are about. It would be the kind of young woman,' she added,
'who likes to be hurt.'

'Do they?' said Vincent, simply.

'Of course. I have remarked it too among American girls, even
– I suppose by reaction – those who have been spoilt by their
men into petty tyrants. If they do, they will get what they want:

they will be horribly treated there. The stories that one hears! Last year it was the great joke to make the tour of all the houses of their families' friends – good people, you know, of the higher bourgeoisie. Then, when they had established themselves, to see how many of the young daughters of the house they could seduce; the one who had accomplished the most being elected a kind of Commissar of the Alcove. But seduction was not considered enough: the girl must become *enceinte*, and then there must be an abortion – and – if possible, her suicide or death. Oh, there was more than one, I assure you; and a charming child I knew is in a madhouse, and another is a cripple for life. Another – again I knew her slightly – was like one hypnotized. She ran away with him, with one of the worst of them, I mean, Blaise Boissevain. He's the cleverest, too. It is said that he sent her out on to the streets to solicit for him. She went, and afterwards killed herself, but very carefully, so as not to compromise him. She left a letter, too, in which she called him the Liberator, and said they were all pioneers of a new civilization. They all, and he especially, have some power over women's minds. They are virile, too, you know. It is not a question of that *"Apostolat pédérastique"* so fashionable a few seasons ago. They leave that to the older men, whom they persecute in a quite particularly detestable way. You know how Frenchmen adore their mothers…' But Vincent was not at the moment interested in the sufferings of homosexual Frenchmen of his own age. 'Blaise' was the sound in his head. 'Blaise. Blaise.' That whisper of a name had passed Cherry's lips. *'You were Blaise's joke.'* That pale slug of a lad had been with her at Miss Van Norden's tea-party, turning, turning round the tables.

'Blaise, Blaise Boissevain. I think I've heard the name. Did you say he was the worst?' 'I think so,' she answered cheerfully. 'His young women usually die one way or another. And, as happens, his gifts are remarkable. He quite openly practises spells, some based on a desecration of the Host. And they work. But I have horrified you, Mr Penrose. You know Paris too well to think that one set of corrupt children can affect, let alone typify our civilization. Only, as you say, wickedness is staged here. It is perhaps safer so.' His answer made her, for the first time, glance at him sharply:

'A girl would stand no chance with him whatever?'

'I'm afraid not. Not if she ever got among them at all. You see, if she did, she would not stay unless she liked that sort of thing; unless it corresponded with some hidden need in her or some taste. You see, they are not particularly attractive physically or well-off. And, *mon Dieu!* they are not kind.'

'Tell me one more thing,' he said slowly. 'Why do they meet at the house of that old Miss Van Norden? I went there and I could not make it out at all.' All the contempt which it is possible for woman to feel for woman was in her answer. She raised her silver shingled head, twisted her pearls, flung out one full, still lovely arm, its nacre skin shining under black lace. He thought of old Miss Van Norden's boots, square like a footballer's, her lank, cropped, iron hair, her shrivelled body in an overall tied round the middle with a twist of cord, her nutmeg-engraved skin.

'The poor old creature! But is not France large enough for all? It is the hunger they have for it, the Americans. She knows nothing of her circle, nothing. She sees herself – into whose eyes no man has ever looked – as the *salonnière* – her house full of young men of genius. And how it amuses them! To be so decorous: to mingle there, as happens, with the innocent, the respectable, the lovers of ancient paintings, the eccentric-art snobs! To go there before some secret party, some dreadful escapade. To leave it – to vanish on strange errands into those ancient palpitating dark streets. They are connoisseurs in their way: to them a bad nut is *"délicieux à croquer"*. If she knew! But she knows nothing. But if I know anything of them, they are preparing for her a charming entertainment. She is a woman of letters, she takes herself seriously. One day she will find herself embroiled in one of their scandals....'
Vincent gathered that, when that happened, at least one woman of Paris would laugh. Soon after he took his leave, with the sincerest thanks, and went for a long walk.

So that was where the girl had been, secretly, all the time. There had been the centre of her life and he had thought her without one; would have given her one. In such a set as that she had found her feet, his young Artemis. There had been her hunting-ground, with such huntsmen – and such a prey. *'Thy chase had a beast in view.'* For an instant he saw himself, as a quarry that had been spared. The thought humiliated, but why had it happened? Some wisp of compassion – of love? Or had Blaise got bored and early called it off? He was not yet in his senses about Cherry, but a reserve of clarity in his nature told him that he would be. Again, he had not wanted a captive, but she a master. And had found it in Blaise. He imagined her intonations when she said *'Blaise'*. Imagined other things. It hurt.

A moment later he reproached himself, thinking: 'I did not love her enough, or I would have saved her. I would have found a way.' Until he could not help hearing the angel of his *'clarté'* saying: 'You are old enough to know that you cannot: that it is impossible. She cannot now eat natural food. She never relished it: she is feeding now on what she likes. No, she was not wholly an evil child, or she would not have spared you at all; would have married you to make sport for Blaise and his crew.' He had the dislike of his kind for the abnormal, though he criticized his distaste, and began to realize again how she had been carried into a world he could never penetrate. Only the utmost height of passion would have given him the power and the insight, and that he had not felt. 'Love one of your own kind,' was the answer of his angel, 'if ever this comes your way again.' He walked fast, striding over a delicate Paris bridge into the darkening afternoon, into the tall shadows of the Left Bank.

Then his mood changed for a moment into a great pity. Pity for the girl, pity also for the boys, caught with their victims in the traps they had set, whose artificial hell was only too likely to turn into a real one. Passionately he wished, as he had often wished, that his own wounds had won a better world for them, a world wherein they would not have found it possible to invent the form of life they had. Then cursed himself for a sentimentalist. Part of this Actæon they had spared would have liked to turn their own dogs on them. Then thought that France might have done better by her most brilliant children. Then that their sickness was part of the world's sickness.

He was not unhappy now, walking in the understanding of the meaning of events, which of all experiences puts suffering and disappointment most in their right places; conquers them, if it can keep them there. *'Rapture of the intellect at the approach of the fact'* this state was called once; and he went on moving in it, until the beginning of fatigue from city-pavement walking pulled him up.

He found that he was not far off from the old woman's house, and an impulse seized him to return there. Cherry might be inside. The thought of a sight of her was still exquisite pain. He would take one last look at her with the knowledge he had gained: one more look at that infernal dance, going on, counter-clockwise round the tables. A first real look and a last, at the people who had taken Cherry away – (was it possible that it might not be the last, that he still had something for Cherry? Could do something for Cherry? Would find a way to take her from Blaise and what Blaise meant?) One more look at the Fragonard, laughing on the wall, work of a saner age. One more look at old Miss Van Norden, who did not know what happened in her house.

He went into the courtyard. The trees were still crying in low voices. He rang the bell. She was at home. Cherry was not there. But it was all going on as it had gone on before, a replica of that day he had brought the girl and of all other days. 'Weave, weave your infernal dance,' his mind murmured. But today they did not seem to be, any of them, the same people; nor could he hear any French spoken, only American. 'They' were not there. Anyhow, it mattered nothing, since Cherry and Blaise were not there.

As before, the room was not lit until it was almost too dark to see; and for some time the noble fire burned by itself, like a giant rose. He had finished his second cup of tea, sitting where he had sat before, with the Fragonard for company. The ancient furniture gleamed, the huge cabinets along the wall repeating the fire in their panels. An ancient servant came in and put a taper to the candles, and the whole room was picked out with gleam and reflection, the repetition of their pointed flames.

As it had been before. One part of his brain had observed for the first time a particular series of brightnesses, which in daylight had been invisible, as if candle, not daylight was needed to pick them out. Again they sprang into being, all round the room, on top or along the higher shelves of the wall-furniture; something in metal, a series, a sequence. He could not determine what they were. His hostess, who had been circling with her guests, came and sat beside him. She poked forward her cropped stringy head at him: 'Seen everything you want to, Mr....?' She spoke shortly. She would not, he saw, welcome stray Englishmen of no particular 'chic', who might be using her house as hunting-ground for a pretty girl. He remembered what the Frenchwoman had said, shared her opinion of the woman. He gave a conventional answer, while she must have seen his eyes straying along the high shelves and the cabinet tops.

'Have you seen those?' she asked. He rose with her and they crossed the room to one of the shining objects, now level with his head. On the next cabinet stood another: and another. They were all the same. About a foot high, of some common metal, gilt, rough, traditional. But the design was pure, the whole representing a flame or a star on fire, inset with a circular disk, rubbed silver-bright and painted on it in blue, the letter Chi. It was clear now what they were: they were frames, supports, stands for the ciborium, the box – in this case a round of hollow glass, fixed on to the disk – to hold the wafers of the Host. The box taken away, they now made delightful chimney-piece ornaments. He saw it for himself and Miss Van Norden explained, and told how they had been sent her from Spain, and had once been part of the traditional altar-furniture in country churches.

'Those Greek letters are the only relic of piety about them,' she added, 'and cleaning will soon wear them off. Interesting parochial baroque – and from the country of its origin too. For they are not old.' She picked up one and began to rub it on a filthy handkerchief of khaki cotton, on which she spat. The old paint was dry and cracked and the signature of Christ rubbed off at a touch.

'I must be going,' he said. 'I only wanted to thank you for showing me your collection. It is superb. I shall never forget it.'

She was looking hard at him. Her head was like one of those carved out of a dark nut. She grinned. In matter of practice it was not the face of one who does not know what is happening in her house. Her contempt for her body, but not for her surroundings, and for all that otherwise makes life worth living, had something enormous about it, as if a rock could fling its shadow evenly around itself in an ever-widening circle. They were standing near the fire. He looked down the whole length of the room. Point after point, the empty flames burned up the boxes which had held the bread of life broken off them. He looked at her again. The old eyes twinkled up at him:

'Two of my little friends, Cherry and her Blaise, aren't here today. They've gone off somewhere. No hope, I fear, of wedding bells. I'm afraid that some of my countrywomen have less morals than your English girls. While Blaise's affairs never last long. Just the conventional change of sweethearts, with a new excuse. It's only his endings that can be called original...'

She had hardly done speaking when his courtesies followed. Walking slowly down the room, touching with his left shoulder or his right the dancers as he passed, his eyes stayed fixed on the stripped stars of the Host. The Frenchwoman had been wrong, but now he understood.

Bellerophon to Anteia

...and when he became hated of all the Gods, he went away...eating his heart.

When all is said and done, I should prefer that you should know, Anteia, how I came to be here. It seems that you have a right to know, since you liked me so much. I thought that I knew what our preference for each other would mean, but here I am in this place where the grasses are grey and the sand white and the dull sea is never quiet or coloured and the wind does not stop.

I cannot stop, but I am going nowhere, and there is nothing but the memory of it to remind me that I hunted the chimæra in mid-air. I knew that, after what happened that day in the corridor at Scyros, I should come to an end of the sun and colours, on dead beaches, and that a spin of sand racing the dunes would be the hero Bellerophon. I do not know why it should be so, only that you took a fancy to me that rich autumn so that I had to go away, even from myself, to dance in the sand, a thin ghost.

In this there is nothing I would have chosen.

Already the wind is fingering me. A hero must be sorely winnowed and withered to be turned so light. When I left you, you will remember, I had on gold armour and a purple crest. I am not wearing them now. I should like to tell you how I got here, how I found the place.

You never know what adventures may lie in caves. I was already half-way up a hill when I saw an entrance where I hoped to find a beast that would engage me in fight. My armour was already a little dull, and I wished to exchange it for a light skin to protect

185

me until I should have found a way out of my exile. There was
nothing in the cave, but some way back water dripping from the
roof. The cave ran low, oiled and green, but stooping I went
under it and found myself in a black hall that glittered. The sand
under my feet sparkled, dry and glorious. I marched, and thun-
dered my name, *Bellerophon*. I honoured that place at least. I saw
myself dipped in dry star-dust. It seemed a day's march through.
At the end there was a small arch and a passage of pebbles and
slow water, a stream two inches deep but not pure. There were
too many green ferns, one could not see out of what soil they
grew. It was certainly daylight. I hurried through.

I stood on stone at the edge of a round pool that was open to
the sky. There was a belt of rocks round it. I could not see over,
but I rubbed, even with my tongue, the dry bloom on the gold
stone, and was then reminded of a terrace at Scyros and of the
painful names given to our intimacy. Then I forgot even these, I
was so pleased with the double circle of sky and water, a blue lid
over a blue plate – I could have broken the plate and eaten it like
cracked sweet ice. I crossed in a bowl floating there, which may
have been the one Herakles left.

After that there was another passage with the same quality of
light as a brown blight gives over a strong sun. It came from one
side, through windows, and there was sometimes a sighing sound.
I went down it indefinitely, until I heard a noise of banging
repeated with a roar between the strokes. It was instantly dark.
There was a cave and up it a sea running from some ocean, on
to a black beach. There was a gleam when the wave ran up, and
a horror to hear it strike, and, as it slid back the suck, suck, on
the stones.

I stripped and leapt upon a breaker, and, parting it with my
hand, rode up, and lay a long time on the beach of black stones
while the water screamed past me. I leapt up the oiled face of
the cliff, and heard the waves mount after me, climbing each
other's backs. Through a hole in the face of the rock, I entered
a hall of unrecognizable gods. I think you might know some of
their names. They were saying: 'There goes the hero Bellerophon,'
but not kindly.

After that I watched confusedly. I remember that I studied in
great expectation some writing that formed itself on a scroll, where

our affair was described in sentences that depended upon a sentence that was not written. I spent some time at this until I fell into disgust. Again, there was much that I should have wished to refer to you.

You will now want to hear the end. I can tell you that. For some time the nature of my walk had changed. There had come a tender light. I particularly remember a green and violet light that sometimes turned rosy; and the ground was spongy but not disagreeable, except through an apprehension of its wetness I could not help feeling. I had known when I entered the ocean cave that it was all up. I could not believe it, of course, but I was surprised when I found at the end a small dry room with a floor of clean sand and at the further side a shelf or an altar cut out of the rock, powdered with clean sand and empty. The light sand on the floor drifted up to it. Later I found a way out on to these beaches.

That is all I have to tell you. Adieu.

Mappa Mundi

Paris is not a safe city. It is never supposed to be, but so often for the wrong reasons. Perhaps the only place in the world that is really and truly both a sink of iniquity and a fountain of life at one and the same time; in the same quarter, in the same place, at the same hour, with the same properties – to even the same person.

It is no use, or not much use, to know it only as a spree, or as an æsthetic jolt, returning very sophisticated about it. Like all the great feminine places, behind its first dazzling free display, you come quickly upon profound reserves. After the spree a veil is drawn, a sober, *noli me tangere* veil. Isis, whose face on a first swift initiation you think you have seen, even to the colour of her eyes, Isis you believe you have kissed, withdraws, well wrapped-up, grown instantly to her own height – as is the property of a goddess. Colossal, as Apuleius saw Hecate, and made of stone which is goddess's material; and for lover and mistress you are left with an image, remote as St Geneviève where she stands looking up stream, an inviolable city behind her.

Properly snubbed, or enchanted, if you remain, above all if you live there, you learn that the delights of that first spree are repeated and confirmed as pleasure does not often repeat itself. Not only these, you find that there are others, possibilities of thrilling ways of life that do not depend on wealth or sex or the excitements between midnight and dawn; vistas of well-being that touch the commonest acts with the service of the Goddess and her law, the quality of sheer living, sufficient in itself, as Tamar Karsavina tells in her book.